BEAR HUG

A MIDNIGHT RISING NOVELLA: THE EIFFEL CREEK SAGA 0.5

THIA MACKIN

AUTHOR'S COPYRIGHT

Bear Hug

Copyright © 2021 *Mackin Works, LLC* and *Thia Mackin*

Excerpt from *Tequila Moon* copyright © 2020 *Mackin Works, LLC* and *Thia Mackin*

ALL RIGHTS RESERVED

Editing by: Meredith Bowery

Cover by: Harvest Moon Designs

Interior Design and Formatting: Harvest Moon Designs

No part of this publication may be reproduced, distributed, or transmitted in any form or by any means, electronic or mechanical, or stored in a database or retrieval system, (other than for review or promotional purposes) without the prior written permission of the author, except for the use of brief quotations in a review.

This book is a work of fiction. Names, characters, businesses, places, events, and incidents are either the products of the author's imagination or used in a fictitious manner. Any resemblance to actual persons, living or dead, or actual events is purely coincidental. The author acknowledges the trademarked status and trademark owners of various products possibly referenced in this work of fiction, which have been used without permission. The use and publication of these trademarks is not authorized, associated with, or sponsored by the trademark owners.

ALSO BY THIA MACKIN

Midnight Rising Novels

The Depths of Winter Trilogy
Hard Frost (Book 1)
Cold Comfort (Book 2)
Frost Burn (Book 3)

The Eiffel Creek Saga
Bear Hug (Standalone Novella)
Tequila Moon

Visit my website at www.thiamackin.com

ACKNOWLEDGMENTS

This story might be short and sweet, but it still needed a village.

As always, to my Alpha reader and co-creator, **Kat Corley**. Finally, she got to read a book with all brand-new-to-her characters and story. If not for the strong foundation we built together, Eiffel Creek and the residents (past, present, and future) would never exist. She also pointed out an important difference between writing a 30,000-word story and a 90,000-word book that helped move the plot along.

To my incredibly supportive beta team—

Barb Jack and **Lisa Simo-Kinzer**, you two single-handedly forced me to add about 2200 additional words with your comments and suggestions, and I like to think the story is better for it; **Jessica Slavik**, I'm sorry Hazel didn't end up with a superhero. I promise that he'll make her immeasurably happy, though. Maybe not as happy as Jason Momoa would make me, but... We can't all win. You three amazing people shaped this book into something (literally) bigger and better than it would have otherwise been.

To my amazing editor and friend, **Meredith Bowery**, who stayed on board despite the big personal happenings in her life. Congratulations, Marine mama! And eternal gratitude to **Christine Sullivan Mulcair** for her oh-so-needed proofread. I have decided that hyphens are the bane of my existence. Thank the gods for her! (Any remaining typos are my fault.)

To **Kallypso Masters**, whose nightly sprints are the only reason I finished this story. Our pandemic, social-distanced write-apart helped me finish a scene that stumped me for days.

Also to **Marisa Scolamiero**, who prevented me from losing my mind these past months. True friends are hard to find, harder to keep, and so damned valuable. You're such an amazing person. Thanks for being part of my life. I'd kidnap CS for you if I could.

While all of our circles shrank during 2020 with the insanity in the world, it will always take a village. I'm incredibly proud of and grateful to mine.

And if I forgot to name you, I'm sorry. I still love you!

~Thia

AUTHORS' NOTE

Dear Readers,

This adventure began in 2005 when two nerdy best friends took a writing prompt and began a universe. We—Kat and Thia—were both avid readers of fantasy and urban fantasy. So when someone invited Thia to do text-based roleplay in an urban fantasy world, she wanted to jump in with both feet! Except... the premise wasn't believable. The creatures were a mishmash from different worlds, and she couldn't suspend her disbelief to enjoy it.

We had always shared our books and ideas, which was what happened as we sat in Kat's bedroom after Kat's graduation party. She agreed. Whoever put it together created it for the "fun" factor, to make it flashy. But... what if paranormals *were* real? What if something pushed them over the edge until they could no longer stand peaceably in the shadows? How could we make people *believe* that vampires, shapeshifters, and other paranormals had remained hidden for so long—and were more powerful than we humans could ever imagine?

So we tore it down to this base idea that paranormals

were going to take over. We established the *What, When, Where,* and *Why.* Then we built the *Who* and *How.* All we had left was… well… everything else. But we pored over legends of established creatures, like vampires, and separated "fact" from fiction. It needed to make sense. There needed to be a scientific or logical basis. We want you to *believe* while you read our stories, enough that you can wander happily lost in the pages.

For about six months between 2005 and 2006, we invited others to play in our world through text-based roleplay. Unfortunately, though the members were phenomenal and we loved them greatly, it didn't feel right to have others creating characters in a world we crafted. So we shut down the ProBoards account after a heartbreaking goodbye and went back to our pre-RP basis before we continued layering, growing, and writing.

On May 25, 2005, Midnight Rising was born. However, it grows daily. Now we invite you to visit—and we hope you stay.

Yours truly,
    Kat Corley and Thia Mackin

To finding the person who doesn't care if you are a bear first thing in the morning, middle of the day, late at night, or the three days of the full moon.

You're worth it.

CHAPTER 1

The crowd still roared in the distance as Hazel "Bear Hug" Metcalf slid into the chair at the center of the long white table. She resisted the urge to move the microphone back. The adrenaline pumping through her veins made her feel crowded, but she knew from past experience it would cause feedback and a couple seconds of chaos if she touched it. With the long tablecloth hiding her from the front, she let her leg bounce to channel the overflow of energy after the recent fight. Soon, the aches and pains would hit, including the gash over her eye and an impressive bruise over her ribs. She hoped they would be on the way to the hotel by then.

Scanning the room, she frowned upon seeing the increased security at the doors. Only people with press passes hanging from their neck sat in the audience, though normally a few VIPs finagled their way in. Before she could overthink it, her manager, David Gonzalez, took the chair beside her and signaled the first reporter to raise his hand. David knew each by name and publication, but Hazel only recognized two—Mack Godram and Chelsea Ives. Mack had been one of two reporters at her first-ever match and win. He'd covered every one since, and they'd even taken to emailing and, more rarely, texting between events. Ms. Ives wanted to do an exclusive exposé on Hazel's sudden appearance and rise in the ranks of the mixed martial arts scene; she'd been hounding the team for months. For everyone else, she repeated the name David used when he called on them.

"Ms. Metcalf, you are one fight away from being World Fighting Inc.'s bantamweight champion. What do you intend to do in the next month to ensure your win?"

"Just the normal after one fight and before another. Recover. Sleep. Train. I'll try not to read the articles predicting my loss and avoid letting those of you promising my win go to my head." She grinned specifically at Mack, as his articles sang her praises. In a group of cutthroat sports journalists, he always treated her with respect and kindness. Plus, he looked yummy in a gruff Clark Kent way. "Then I hope I fight better than current Bantamweight Champion Michaela Quinn. She's incredibly talented, heck of a fighter, and has more experience than I do in the circuit. I'm blessed to even face her in the octagon."

David called on the next reporter, working his way around the room.

"How do you feel about the bigger organizations recently buying up the smaller ones? Do you think WFI is next?"

Hazel looked in the direction of the question. "The owners of WFI have given a lot of female MMA fighters the opportunity to showcase our abilities, and I hope we continue that trend in the future. However, it's a business. I have to stay in tip-top shape and win, and WFI has to adjust with the times. Until other organizations give additional coverage to women in the sport, I'll be grateful for the chances that World Fighting Inc. affords me."

"Tell us about this stalker the tabloids mention," another ordered.

Hazel snapped to attention, realizing that the increased security and smaller crowd meant something had happened today while she was fighting. However, David waved that question away and answered before she could reveal too much. Hazel hated deflecting questions, not wanting to disappoint anyone. "There is an active investigation, and we cannot discuss any details at this time."

Hazel casually bumped her elbow against her manager and friend's arm in thanks.

Finally, David called on Mack.

"How's your eye, Hazel? That elbow should have disqualified her," he began, the corner of his mouth twisting in disapproval as he leaned forward in his chair. Even from twenty feet away, she recognized the worry in his brown-green eyes and the concern wrinkling his forehead.

Hazel shrugged a shoulder, her blue eyes alight at how much he cared. She wanted to smooth his black hair down as she reassured him. "The referee made the right call. It wasn't an intentional eye gouge. However, I look forward to some peace and quiet, because that strike rang my bell a bit. Thank you for asking."

"Has your trainer formed a strategy for avoiding Michaela Quinn's left hook? Her last five fights have ended in knockouts in under thirty-five seconds." Mack didn't even look at his notes, as though he'd practiced his question before it came around to him.

"Vin Diaz has the same strategy every fight. 'Duck and weave, move your feet!'" Hazel grinned, hearing her trainer's gruff voice in her head. "It hasn't failed me yet."

David stood and thanked the reporters. "We look forward to seeing you all in three weeks at the pre-fight conference."

Taking his lead, Hazel waved at the group and thanked

4 | THIA MACKIN

them all. Then she followed him off the stage and through the door. When it closed behind them, locking all the strangers away and leaving her alone in the hallway with her team, she exhaled in relief. Then her trainer tossed her jacket toward her.

"Duck and weave," Vin muttered, waiting until she passed to step in behind her. "That's something that any trainer could tell you!"

Hazel paused, wrapping her arm around her longtime friend's shoulder. They'd celebrated his fifty-eighth birthday earlier this year, but he moved like someone half his age. She hoped he'd still be training her at eighty. "No one can show me how to do it as effectively as you, though. It isn't the words that help me win. It's the technique, and I can only get that from you."

Vin's wiry body deflated, his arm pulling her close to hug her back. "You did good out there, Hazel. The match would have been over at least fifteen seconds sooner if that elbow hadn't caught you. Surprisingly, I agree with that journalist. They should have disqualified her for gouging. We are going to have to get X-rays to make sure she didn't damage the orbital cavity."

Ahead of them and guarding the exit where their vehicle would be waiting, Barry Litgram waited. He served as her bodyguard and physical trainer. "I thought you hired me to make medical decisions?" he asked, opening the building door seconds before David led the way out.

As they'd rehearsed dozens of times since the stalker sent the first threat, David opened the rear passenger door for Hazel to slide across to buckle up behind the driver. Vin followed her in, cutting between the bucket seats and into the third row while David opened and climbed into the front seat. Barry shut the venue door and joined Hazel in the middle, closing the SUV door and barking to the driver that everyone was clear. He continued scanning the crowd, on higher alert than normal.

Immediately, the SUV went into motion as the passengers finished buckling in. Their eyes recovered quickly from the paparazzi's flashbulbs as the driver merged into traffic and headed toward the hotel. Barry and David reminded her constantly that the transfer from the building to the vehicle was the most dangerous time. The blinding lights and loud noises distracted from real threats. Today, though, her team felt more tense than normal, and she wondered why until Vin spoke up from the back seat.

"How is the investigation going? Any update on the stalker?" Vin asked, concern in his voice. "I heard all of our gear had to be moved from one hotel to another while Hazel and I were warming up. Did they pull any fingerprints?"

For the first time, genuine fear filled her as the situation became more real. Up to now, there'd only been letters, phone calls, and the occasional long-distance threat. If he'd found their hotel rooms… Hazel twisted in the seat, her teeth worrying her bottom lip. "Maybe we need to postpone the fight. His last letter threatened all of you. Nothing is worth endangering you guys."

Barry lightly punched her arm, his brotherly affection keeping him from worsening any bruises. "What? You don't think we can handle one little stalker?"

Hazel rolled her eyes with a laugh. "Down, boy. I'm not casting aspersions on your machismo, but I'd never want any of you injured for something as ridiculous as a fight. A championship is not life or death; we can go for it again next year after they find the guy. *Your* lives *matter* to me."

Vin patted her shoulder from the back. "And that's why we are in your corner, Hazel. We're family."

David turned in his seat and looked meaningfully at Vin. Hazel glanced between them. "What?"

Her manager grinned sheepishly. "After you're the new bantamweight champion, we have something important to…"

He paused, alarm changing the expression on his face as he looked over her shoulder. Hazel glanced to her left, seeing headlights much too close. Between one second and the next, her eyes noticed the pavement closer to her head than the night sky. Then the streetlights. Then the ground. Then everything went dark.

"Hazel. Hazel!" David shouted, kneeling over her and touching her face. "Hazel, open your eyes. I need you to open your eyes."

Choking on liquid in her throat, Hazel forced herself to listen. She looked up into his heartbroken brown eyes. She tried to raise her hand to touch his face, but nothing worked and everything hurt.

"Hazel, you are losing too much blood, and I can smell blood pooling under the skin of your abdomen. The ambulance won't be here in time. I can try to save your life, but nothing will ever be the same again if this works. You have to choose. Please say yes. It's a yes or no, Hazelbear."

He looked inconsolable as he stared down at her. She trusted him, even if she didn't understand what he meant. How could she say no?

As she tried to form the words, only blood and spittle came out, and she choked harder. So she nodded.

"Thank fuck," he whispered. "Close your eyes a second, little cub. Rest a minute."

Resting sounded good. She closed her eyes, only to hear an animal-like grunting noise nearby. A vise clamped down over the shredded skin of her arm. Her eyes opened as she tried to scream in agony and drowned on her own blood. A dark-colored bear stood above her with his jaws worrying at her forearm. Massive, he appeared to be the size of the crumpled SUV.

"Goddamn it, David, what are you doing?" Vin half-shouted, climbing out of the wreckage. "She won't survive the change!"

Barry walked toward the bear, his body language calm despite the massive creature pointing its bloody snout in his direction. If he wasn't worried, she shouldn't be either, Hazel's thoughts reasoned. "Her stalker is dead. His scent matched the one in her hotel room. I broke his neck. It'll look like it happened in the crash. How's our girl?"

"Dying," Vin whispered, kneeling on her other side and gripping her hand in his. "Hey, Hazelbear, we love you. You brought together three grumpy Ursus and made us arktoi—a family."

Hazel smiled softly, blood-covered lips turning up. Then her eyes closed, and the sounds of a bear bellowing in pain filled her ears.

A COOL DRAFT TOUCHED HAZEL'S FACE, AND SHE OPENED HER eyes to a bright, white light. Outside, sunlight reflected off mounds of snow, blinding her until she pulled the top cover over her head. Groaning, she stretched her tight muscles. Had she gone to bed without a hot shower and her tub of Icy Hot?

"Hazel, you awake?" Vin called through the door, knocking softly.

Uncovering her head, she blinked as she studied the room. While she often woke up in strange rooms as they hopped from one hotel to another, this was definitely a cabin. However, it only took her another second to realize that this wasn't their normal getaway cabin. Usually, they trained in the Smoky Mountains, but this place smelled different. Stronger. Weirdly, every smell seemed more distinct. The dozens of scents were overwhelming. Also, the Smokies didn't normally have this much snow when they visited.

"I'm awake," she croaked, raising the covers to check that she hadn't slept in the nude.

The oversized flannel pajamas made her comfortable slipping her feet over the side of the bed and sitting up. However, she held still as her head swam. Raising a hand to her face, she felt overly warm. Also, the gash in her eyebrow from her opponent's accidental elbow had healed without even a scab.

Weird.

The door opened, and Vin entered with a steaming cup of hot chocolate. He watched her, worry wrinkling his brow, as he handed over the mug. She grinned at him, ignoring his concern as she noticed the heap of mini marshmallows on top.

"You're a lifesaver!" she murmured, raising it cautiously to her lips to sip. Her eyes closed in pleasure at the strong chocolate taste cut by the melty, sugary sweetness of the marshmallows.

He patted her leg, sitting on the mattress beside her. His hand stayed on her leg, and she realized it was more for his reassurance than hers. The silence drew out until she set the cup on the nightstand. "Out with it, mister."

"Hazel," he paused, visibly bracing himself before continuing, "do you remember the accident? Do you remember the wreck?"

Hazel's brow wrinkled. Thinking back, she remembered talking with the press, going to the SUV, and worrying about security changing their hotel. Then headlights, excruciating pain, and...

"There was a bear?" she whispered then shook her head, doubting her own memory.

Vin sighed. "Yes, there was a bear. But... Why don't you get dressed and come to the kitchen? Just follow your nose," he urged with a half-hearted smile.

She grabbed his hand and squeezed, causing him to wince slightly. "Hey. Is everyone okay? David and Barry?"

He released her hand and stood. "They are the same as ever. Waiting in the kitchen. And we have another visitor. Just come out when you're ready."

Once he closed the door behind him, Hazel quickly opened the closet and found her suitcase. Pulling out the warmest items she'd packed, she dressed and hunted for her shoes. She brushed her tangled hair with a wince then quickly braided it back, not taking the extra time to French braid it. Her heart beat double-time, worried by Vin's morose demeanor. Something was very wrong.

Checking herself in the mirror, she made sure she'd buttoned everything up properly in her hurry. Then she grabbed the cup of hot chocolate, opened the door, and headed toward the kitchen. As Vin had said, she followed her nose. Hints of bacon, sausage, and pancakes permeated the air. The growl of her stomach as she stopped in the kitchen doorway reminded her of the bear at the crash.

A bear in Las Vegas? She snorted at her own imagination, facing the four people sitting at the kitchen table. The stranger, probably in his mid to late forties, stood as she entered—causing Vin, Barry, and David to follow his lead. "Hello, Hazel Metcalf. My name is Paolo Cerutti. It is a pleasure to meet you."

He gestured to the fifth chair at the table, and Barry took a heaping plate of pancakes covered in butter off the stove to set in front of her. "Mr. Cerutti, it's a pleasure to meet you also."

Hesitantly, she stepped forward and slipped into the chair between Paolo and Vin. She'd much rather have sat beside someone other than the stranger, but she didn't want to be rude. Besides, something about the man felt powerful, like a member of the mob who expected everyone to do exactly as he said. Once she sat, everyone else did too.

Nervously, she picked up her fork to cut into the pancakes. Though she avoided meat, the smell of bacon in the air caused her mouth to water. The guys would definitely think she had a head injury if she asked for a plate of it. Instead, she cut another bite of pancake, looking around for the syrup but not wanting to offend the stranger by interrupting him to find it.

"Ms. Metcalf, may I call you Hazel?" At her nod, he smiled. "And please call me Paolo. Hazel, you are quite the miracle."

Chewing her third forkful of pancakes, she stopped self-consciously as everyone looked her way. "I'm only as good as the people around me."

The stranger chuckled, upping her discomfort. "Truer than you know. Vincent says you remember a bear after the wreck? What else do you remember?"

Hazel set the fork back on her plate and rubbed her hand on the napkin under the knife, suddenly nauseous. "A lot of pain. Everything hurt. And a lot of blood. Was the bear a hallucination caused by blood loss?"

Paolo shook his head. "No, Hazel. The bear was David. You were dying, and he took a great risk to try to save you. Do you remember him asking permission to turn you?"

Hazel glanced toward David, who stared at the table. "What do you mean 'turn me'?"

Her brain stuttered, and she looked at Vin then Barry—both of them watching her with a message in their eyes she couldn't understand. She strained to comprehend what they were trying to convey.

"Hazel, dear, look at me please," the stranger requested, compelling her obedience. Though she turned her head toward him, she closed her eyes to concentrate.

"David... he did say something." Thinking back, she flipped through the broken images and battered memories. "I —it's hard to remember. He asked me to say yes to something. It could save my life but change everything. My choice. And I nodded."

Opening her eyes, she caught the relief on everyone's face except Paolo's. He simply watched her. "Thank you. I know that was difficult. After you nodded, that is when the bear appeared?"

Hazel crumpled the napkin. "That's when I thought I saw the bear, yes."

"And you no longer saw David?" She shook her head in reply. "Because he became the bear."

Hazel glanced at her longtime friend and manager in disbelief. Then she laughed. "The only time David is a bear is when he doesn't get at least six hours of sleep or after a late party."

Paolo rested his hand on the table, and she met his gaze as though forced. "David is an Alpha Ursus. He becomes a bear on the three nights of the full moon and anytime he actively chooses to shift. Which he did in the middle of a city after your accident, because he hoped that changing you would save your life. He bit you. Do you remember?"

The earlier sense of doom returned, causing her heart to race as her breaths turned to pants. "David is not a bear. And I'm not going to be a bear."

Paolo held his hand out to Hazel, but she glanced sideways toward David. After a moment, David extended his hand to her, and she instantly took it. His fingers felt cold and clammy, as though this meeting made him nervous, but he nodded to her and squeezed her hand. Then he placed her hand on Paolo's. Instantly, her breathing evened out.

The stranger smiled softly. "Yes, he is. And we hope you will be. Because the virus—which he passed to you through his bite—has already taken hold. It healed the injuries from the accident, though it should have killed you. You were already weakened by blood loss, and if someone is dying, normally the virus doesn't affect them before they pass. Over the next three weeks, you are going to feel like you have a bad flu. Then you are going to fall into a coma. Either you will awake and shift for the first time, or you will die."

I will die? she thought, shocked and still putting the pieces back together. "The stalker hit us? What about our driver? Did he make it?"

Vin hesitated. "Your stalker is dead, but unfortunately, the driver was human. He died instantly."

Her mind spun as tears filled her eyes, the memory of the crash strengthening as they all talked. "What's an arktoi?" Hazel asked, gripping the stranger's hand to ground herself as she remembered Vin whispering to her as she lay dying.

"That will probably be more confusing than the rest of this. Each strain of the virus has their own words. Those of us who shift into bears are Ursus. Our groups are called arktoi, like wolves have packs. Vincent leads a small arktoi; he is that group's Abilo. He is nobility among the Ursus, as are all the leaders I appoint. I am the Bruin, the monarch who rules all Ursus. Do you understand?"

One of the tears escaped as Hazel looked at Vin. To the depths of her soul, she knew her friend would never lie to her. "Is this true?" she asked, meeting his eyes and not looking away.

"It is true," he confirmed, his voice breaking.

"When David said it would change everything, he meant

that I would start turning into a bear each month?" she stuttered, having trouble making herself say the words.

"Yes," David confirmed. "Three days a month."

Hazel swallowed. "Okay. So, if I survive the c-coma, I'll be an Ursus in an arktoi with an abuelo—"

"Abilo," Barry corrected.

"With an Abilo who answers to the Bruin?"

Paolo squeezed her hand lightly, reminding her that she hadn't pulled away. "Yes, Hazel. That's exactly correct."

"If I live, I'll turn into a bear, but I won't be able to fight again. If he hadn't bitten me, I'd definitely be dead?"

Paolo nodded, patting their joined hands with his free one. "You'll be able to fight again eventually. First, you have to make it through the change, though. You'll be stronger and faster than when you were fully human, so you'll need to learn to pull your punches to keep from accidentally killing your opponent. Also, you'll need to make sure your blood or saliva doesn't mix with your opponent's. Though Ursus have a low contagion rate compared to Lykos—wolves—there is still the chance you could infect someone after you've been one of us for a while."

Hazel patted his hand back. "Thank you for explaining, but you are wrong. Fighting someone if I'm unnaturally stronger and faster would be unfair. It wouldn't be right. Also, any chance of infecting someone without letting them make the choice I was given would be terrible. I won't do that."

Paolo smiled softly, pulling his hands back and standing. "Hazel, I do hope you become one of us. We will be blessed to have one as kind as you in our ranks. Vincent will call me when the time comes, and I will come back to help you through the change."

He put on his thick down jacket and left through the

front door. After an engine started and the vehicle drove away, the four sat in silence for long minutes.

"I'm sorry," David whispered, head bowed.

She scooted toward him and gripped his fingers in hers. "I made the decision. A different life will be better than no life, right?"

Vincent scooted her plate back in front of her. "You need to eat and keep up your strength. Later, David will shift again, and you can see an Ursus while conscious. Then we'll figure out what we need to tell the media about your sudden disappearance... Until you have full control of your animal self, you won't be able to be in the public eye like you were."

Hazel agreed, though she remembered the doubt in Paolo's eyes that she'd survive the shift.

Quite the miracle, he'd said. *It should have killed you.*

You will shift, or you will die.

An hour later, hugging herself in her bedroom, she couldn't decide which she preferred.

CHAPTER 2

Her teeth chattered as she hugged herself for warmth. Though Vin had moved her chair as close to the fire as possible, David had wrapped her legs in a heated blanket, and Barry had used a king-sized comforter to burrito her in, she couldn't get warm. Quite the change from this morning when her three friends had barely convinced her she couldn't throw herself naked into the tallest snowbank to cool off.

"Two more days," Hazel muttered, glaring at David as he offered her a room temperature bottle of water and a protein shake for lunch.

"Hydrate," he urged. "Only one more day. Tomorrow is the first day of the full moon."

For a minute, panic caught her breath in her chest until the burn in her lungs reminded her to exhale. Tonight then. Tonight, she'd fall into a coma. Within three days, she'd either turn into a bear or die. Most likely, her team—her friends—would have to report to the world that she died of her injuries after the crash.

"Whatever happens, this isn't your fault," Hazel reminded

David for the hundredth time. She wiggled and tugged until her arm came free of her blankets, reaching toward him. Instead of grabbing the bottled water or shake, she snagged his wrist to pull him close.

Bending over, David hugged her tightly. His chin rested on top her head, not wanting her to see him cry. However, she could smell the salty tears filling his eyes. "We love you, Hazelbear. You have to come through this, so I can apologize every full moon for the insane amount of hair you'll sprout and not be able to shave. If you do, I'll tell you how sorry I am that you'll crave red meat and ruin your vegetarian streak every month." He held her tighter as her arm wrapped around his back. "You have to."

Someone knocked loudly on the door, causing him to squeeze once before letting go. "Probably the Bruin. He promised to come back since he lives close. Besides, you are kind of a big deal, being famous and all."

He opened the door, revealing Paolo bundled against the cold Colorado night. "Good evening, Hazel. How are you feeling?"

His eyes expressed concern, trying to examine her beneath the layers of covers. Stopping just inside to let David shut and latch the door, Paolo pulled off his gloves and stuffed them in his pocket. Then he removed his coat and hung it on the coat tree. Once he stomped his boots to eliminate most of the snow, he bent over to unlace and remove them.

"Like I have the worst flu of my life and the most worried mother hens caring for me," she teased softly.

Paolo snorted, carefully stepping around the discarded snow to avoid getting his wool socks wet. "Well, they have been through this before, so who better to 'mother' you through it? Unfortunately, the virus that causes the change has much more lasting effects than a bout of the flu."

He grabbed one of the chairs nearby and picked it up without effort, carrying it closer to Hazel. "Has your Abilo or the members of your arktoi talked to you about what it will mean to be Ursus?"

Hazel accepted the water this time when David offered. She'd learned a few things, like that it was easier to shift if the clothes were removed first. Having lived in close quarters with the guys and considering them all family, seeing them strip down hadn't affected her as much as how massive they were when they shifted. "Not much. I saw them turn, and we talked about how it feels." She smiled ruefully after drinking a third of the bottle. "Also that I probably won't enjoy being a vegetarian as much."

Paolo wrinkled his nose, almost smiling. "You—the person you are, your beliefs, your sense of right and wrong—won't be compromised by the change. You will still be Hazel Metcalf, through and through. However, you'll be exposed to new ideas and new things that you probably never even dreamed existed. Sometimes, new knowledge does revise how or what we think."

She drew her arm back inside the covers, clutching the water bottle to her chest for comfort. "What do you mean?"

He grinned at her. "Nothing as dire as what you seem to be thinking. Before you learned that there are strains of reptile therianthropes—called Sauria—would you ever pass by a sign that says, 'Stay away from the edge; here there be crocodiles,' and think, 'Oh, that crocodile might have been human last month'?"

"Never," Hazel admitted, trying to imagine. "Of course, werewolves were like vampires in my head! Imaginary."

His lips tightened, and the grin faded at the edges. "You mean, like unicorns."

A little panic crept into her voice, though she tried to

keep her expression neutral. "Vampires are real? Are you saying I could be turned and crave red meat *and* blood?!"

Paolo rubbed his hand over his face and coughed. "Fear not. You can only catch one strain of the Thalassemian-Therianthro Virus. Once you go bear, there's no going back."

Suddenly burning alive, Hazel flipped the heated blanket off. To keep her hands busy, she began folding it. "The Thala-whatchama..."

"Thalassemia is a severe form of anemia, and Therianthropy is the ability to change from human to animal. There are two strains of the virus. One turns you into a vampire, and the other turns you into an animal. Unlike the flu, you can only catch one strain, and only humans can catch the virus at all."

Hazel inhaled sharply, and her left eye twitched. She opened her mouth, closed it, and then moved her chair to the opposite side of Paolo's... away from the fire. She carefully scooted all the way back in the chair before asking slowly, "What, exactly, do you mean by 'only humans'?"

Paolo exhaled and muttered something in another language that she didn't hear. It might have been Italian, which made the most sense in her head considering his name. After a moment, though, he switched to English. "I forget that you were completely unEnlightened—knowing nothing of the paranormal world, I mean—before David bit you. However, we are going to make that a conversation for another day. For now, I want you to become most familiar with what you will become."

Her brain accepted that explanation as she felt overwhelmed by all the new information. This was all too much, especially when she wasn't at one hundred percent. Heck, she might not even survive this, and if she didn't, none of this would matter anyway!

"Ursus don't have many species strains left. Just black and

brown bears," David added, still hovering at the edge of the room. "I'm a brown bear, so you will be too."

Hazel pouted a moment. "No polar bears? Or red pandas? How many species of wolves are there?"

Paolo held up a hand. "No. Besides, red pandas are more closely related to weasels than to bears. Lykos have seven sub-strains. However, they also have the most contagious form of the virus. Scientists in our community believe that the number of surviving strains of the virus is directly linked to the level of contagion. Other Ursus strains effectively went extinct due to difficulty spreading them in the human population."

Hazel yawned. Then she covered her mouth in alarm. "It isn't you! I'm not bored! And all of this has me so excited that my heart is pumping a hundred miles a minute. I'm not sure how I can even be tired, honestly."

Paolo scooted his chair closer to hers, reaching out to take her hand. "I'm not offended. It's been a joy discussing this with someone new, especially someone as bighearted as you. Even when we do have new Ursus, it isn't often that I get to be the one teaching them about our world. Usually, the new shifter is bitten in a controlled environment after careful planning and a lot of education."

Hazel willingly took his hand between both of hers, her breathing rapid as though she'd run through the snow to get there. "This isn't what I expected, but I'm glad I made this choice. Honestly, other than the fever and cough, this has been the most relaxing stretch I've had in a long time. I've enjoyed the extra time with my group, my arktoi, even if it is borrowed." She paused, suddenly worried for this new friend. "If you are responsible for all the Ursus, do you have your own arktoi? Do you get to have your own family?"

"One moment, sweetheart," Paolo murmured without

dropping her hand, turning his head toward the back of the cabin. "Vincent, Barry, please come here."

Against the wall, David stood straighter, watching his Bruin intently for some sign. Hazel smiled at him, trying to help him relax. Movement in the back of the cabin almost distracted her from Paolo answering her earlier question. "I do have my own arktoi. My group is larger than this one, but most Ursus form smaller groups than Lykos or other pack-based strains. Ursus do better alone than Lykos, though a small arktoi is better than none. Your arktoi is modest but strong."

She yawned again, leaning forward in her chair to try to stay awake. "Isn't that more work for you, though? More arktoi so more... leaders who answer to you?"

"More arktoi do mean more Abilos, but in the long run, it is less work for me, because the groups have less infighting and build a healthier bond. It all works out in the grand plan."

Vin, Barry, and David stood together near the fireplace, waiting for their monarch to acknowledge them. Hazel gestured to them before covering her mouth again. This time, her eyes watered when she opened them.

"Gentlemen, I'll step outside while you all say good... night. Hazel's going to fall asleep soon," Paolo advised, moving to the door to put his boots back on.

As soon as his back was to her, her friends converged on her. Barry swiped the back of his hand across his eyes, and Hazel tsked him. "Hey, this was the most fun we've had together in a year! You've never let me spar with you before! Who knew you had moves?" she teased.

He grunted. "Hazelbear, I am your *bodyguard*. How exactly did you think I was going to protect you?"

She raised an eyebrow. "With your gun?"

BEAR HUG | 21

Suddenly, he wrapped her in a tight hug. "Come out the other side. We won't be the same if you don't."

Pressing her yawn into his shoulder, she squeezed him tight. "I love you, Barry. Thanks for stopping that evil man from hurting anyone else," she murmured, still sad that stopping the stalker had required taking his life. Heartbroken for their driver who hadn't deserved such a terrible end.

Barry stepped back, kneeling down beside her chair, and David leaned over to hug her. "I'm sorry, Bear Hug. I'm so sorry."

She kissed his cheek, pulling him close and fighting hard to keep her eyes open. "I'm not. Thank you for giving me this extra time. Thank you all for staying with me and covering for me. You all are strong and wonderful. You're gonna be fine, no matter what. You made my bonus time the best of my life, even better than those thirty seconds right after the referee calls me a winner and raises my arm in the center ring."

Vin sniffled, trading places. "That's pretty damn good then," he agreed. "Hazelbear, you don't have a choice. Sleep now, but you better wake up and run with us before the full moon ends. You understand me?" he asked, smoothing down her hair in a fatherly gesture and kissing the top of her head.

"You got it, Papa Bear," she murmured in the middle of a yawn. "You got it."

Vin held on even as he felt her body relax. After a long moment, he lifted her into his arms and carried her to the couch across the room. David brought the blankets, and Barry carried two of the chairs.

Once they'd covered her, her little family settled in to watch and wait.

To find out if their Goldilocks would sleep forever or wake up to turn into a bear like them.

CHAPTER 3

Mack Godram slammed the office phone receiver down, picked it up, and slammed it down again. His office mate, Robert Kyle, peeked over his computer monitor and raised an eyebrow.

"Everything okay over there?"

Mack leaned back in his chair and threw his arm over his eyes. "They canceled the pre-fight news conference."

Though his buddy only covered the sports with "ball" in the name, Robert still winced in sympathy. He knew the score. "Then the fight is going be next."

"The fight is next. They won't have the champion in the ring without a chance for widespread publicity, especially in Las Vegas where they want to drive up gambling debt." He drummed his pencil against his desk calendar, staring at the date he'd circled months ago.

For a long moment, Robert let him process the news. "Did you see the…"

"Yeeeesss," Mack hissed, setting his pencil down before he snapped it. "Tabloids are the worst."

"I mean, a murderous stalker and a bear! How could the *Vegas Investigator* not run the story?"

Mack dropped his arm and turned his head to glare at his buddy. "They talk about a bear that a witness tripping on acid saw at the scene, but they can't tell us who responded to the wreck to take Hazel and her team to the hospital or which hospital or who was admitted or anything actually important. And Hazel hasn't responded to any of the emails or text messages I've sent checking on her."

Robert grinned. "It's adorable that you call *her* Hazel but all the other fighters by their last names."

Mack shook his head, knowing Robert believed just being a celebrity gave people the right to call them whatever they wanted. "Until the fighters give me permission, I am not going to presume to use their first names. She gave me permission. Also, you completely ignored my rant!"

Robert rolled his chair out from behind his desk to where he could look directly at Mack. "Let's be serious for a minute. What is it about Hazel 'Bear Hug' Metcalf that has you so invested? In the three years that we've shared an office, you have never cared personally about any athlete. What makes her different?"

"I like most of the athletes I cover." Mack shrank under Robert's condemning glare. "Okay. But you haven't met her. She's..." He hesitated, searching for the right description.

"Gorgeous? Fit? Able to put you in a coma with a single punch?"

The expression on Mack's face should have shamed Robert into silence for a week. "No. I mean, yes, she could definitely knock me out in under fifteen seconds. She is also an incredibly attractive woman. But that describes every female MMA fighter in the circuit. What sets Hazel apart is that she is... chronically nice, good-hearted, and caring."

Robert rolled his eyes and sent his chair back toward his

desk with a single push. "They are being recorded. Of course they act nice for the cameras. C'mon, Mack."

Holding up a middle finger, not his ring finger, he said, "No, Bob. The night of her first fight, I walked through the hall toward the press room. You know how it is when you are reviewing your notes? I ran into her. If her manager hadn't caught her, she would have landed on her butt at my feet. When I apologized, she apologized. She told me, 'It takes two people to cause an accident.' She introduced herself, and we exchanged names. Her manager rushed her, and she delayed him long enough to let me know it was a pleasure to meet me and sorry she had to bump and run. Then, at the press conference after her first ever fight and win with WFI, she called on me by name." He leaned forward. "She probably met three hundred people that day, and she made sure to remember the name of a nobody in the hallway. None of the other fighters would have done that!"

Robert wiggled his eyebrows suggestively. "Maybe she thought you would be fun to ground and pound."

Mack rubbed his hand over his eyes, feeling resigned. "You really don't understand. Hazel is talented, intelligent, and kind. She deserves to be the bantamweight champion, and some psychopath may have ended her shot at that. Perhaps the reason the only place dropping stories about her is some tabloid is because she's paralyzed—or worse, dead— and her team isn't ready for it to get out."

"Sure, Mack. Or the bear carried her off into the mountains where she plans to live out the rest of her life away from the lights and cameras. Besides, if she is paralyzed or dead, she's not your concern anymore. You are a sports reporter, not an investigative reporter."

Mack exhaled. Although Robert technically told the truth, he genuinely worried about Hazel and hoped she was well. Hopefully, she'd reappear on the scene soon.

BEAR HUG | 25

. . .

TWO WEEKS LATER, THE HOUSE LINE RANG ON THE OPPOSITE side of his home, and Mack groaned, rolling over in bed to look at the clock on his nightstand. 6:30 a.m. *What sadistic jerkwad would call at such an ungodly hour?* he wondered as he slipped out of bed and stumbled toward his kitchen.

The caller ID showed his boss's phone number, and he leaned his head against the doorjamb as he answered. "This is Godram."

"Pack your bag. You're headed to Colorado. Your flight boards at 8:30. I have a car on the way to pick you up and drop you at the airport." The familiar voice was clipped, no-nonsense.

"Good morning, Mr. Henry. Yes, I was sleeping well. No, I had no intention of leaving the state this week. I look forward to seeing you in your office at ten, my normal time."

For a moment, the other end of the phone held static. "Godram, move your ass. Hazel 'Bear Hug' Metcalf is ready to give an exclusive, and you're the reporter she requested. If you blow this for us, you can find yourself another home for your column. The car will be there any minute. Don't keep them waiting."

The line beeped as his boss disconnected, but Mack didn't bother to call him back. Shit. If the man had led with "Hazel Metcalf wants you to interview her in Colorado," he would have put on his gym shoes and started the eight hundred-plus mile trip on foot.

Running up the stairs, he pulled out his suitcase and tossed it on the bed.

"I didn't do laundry. Why didn't I do laundry?" His mutters fell on empty air as he hunted through his drawers for enough clean clothes to get him through a... *How long am I going to be gone? And did he book me a hotel?* Once he made it safely through security, he'd have to call his boss back for more details. For now, he stuffed a variety of warm clothes and his one suit into the suitcase before heading to the bathroom for his essentials.

He pulled his comfortable jeans and a soft button-up shirt out of the closet to wear on the plane. Dressing quickly, he finger-combed his hair before hunting for a clean pair of socks and his shoes. Then he remembered that Colorado was frigid. He needed a jacket. Where did he leave his jacket two years ago when they had that cold spell?

In front of the house, a loud honk sounded. His neighbors were going to murder that driver, he decided as he stuffed the jacket inside and zipped up the suitcase. On his way out the door, he grabbed his briefcase and keys off the kitchen table.

Luckily, the lines moved quickly at the airport. He handed over his suitcase, relieved he no longer had to lug it around. If this was an overnight trip, he'd overpacked. Which reminded him that he needed to call his boss back for additional details, things he hadn't thought to ask about after the purpose of the trip had been revealed.

At the gate, he stepped away from the half-asleep group of travelers waiting for boarding to begin and called his boss's cell phone directly. "What?" Mr. Henry growled, the sounds of a morning radio show in the background.

"Good morning. Thank you for this opportunity."

"Godram..."

"Where am I going? How long am I staying? Do you have the address of my hotel? When am I meeting with Ms. Metcalf?" Mack recognized that warning growl and listed off his questions quickly before his boss hung up on him.

"Somewhere in the middle of nowhere. I don't fucking remember. Her manager is going to pick you up from the airport after you land, and you'll be staying at the cabin they rented, because middle of nowhere doesn't have a hotel. You'll arrange everything with the manager then. Now I'm pulling into the parking garage. You're welcome. Don't fuck this up."

The line went dead, and Mack sighed then grinned as he found a seat where he could spread out and begin his notes for the article. By the time he boarded and the flight attendant handed him a coffee, he had a full page of questions. Some he would eliminate once he saw her. A few he put question marks in front of to assess later whether they were too insensitive. He took a long moment to stare out the window at the Rocky Mountains as the plane began its final descent, then he checked his notes one last time and began packing them away. As he waited for his luggage upon landing less than two hours after takeoff, he felt ready to write the most important article he'd ever been assigned.

However, the expression on her manager's face as Mack slid into the front passenger seat of the SUV seemed anything except pleased. After they cleared the complicated airport roads and merged onto the interstate, he went for an ice breaker. "Thank you for picking me up, and thank you for choosing me for this opportunity."

David Gonzalez growled as he signaled to change lanes. "She's not ready for an interview, but she's not going to get any peace to heal until it happens. Hazel may need to take breaks for no obvious reason, and she tires easily right now. If you overstep or push her past her limits, I will kick you out in the nearest snowdrift to hike forty miles back to town. Do you understand?"

Mack nodded, understanding her manager's protective attitude. He'd feel the same if their positions were reversed. He decided to put David's mind at ease. "I will respect Hazel's needs. I know this may sound strange, but I've been worried about her. The lack of updates about her recovery and what it entails left a lot of her fans at loose ends."

David glanced over at him, his lip curled slightly. He snarled, "You think she owes you and the world more of herself?"

The conversation had gone off the rails. "Of course she doesn't owe a bunch of strangers anything!"

Putting on his hazard lights, David coasted to a stop in the emergency lane. Concerned, Mack did an assessment of his chances of surviving being told to get out. His jacket was lying across the backseat, within reach, but his gloves and scarf were in his suitcase in the back hatch. Worse, his shoes definitely weren't made for hiking the four miles back to the city.

Instead, though, David opened his door and walked to the back bumper. He took off at a fast clip down the road before turning and walking back to the driver's door. After a brief hesitation, David opened the door, climbed back in his seat, and leaned his head against the headrest with his eyes closed.

"Look. You've always been pleasant to Hazel, and I think that you were the best choice to interview her, but the past two months have been really difficult. That dickbag almost killed her, and he did kill an innocent man who had a wife and daughter. She's had to relearn how to do things that she took for granted in her everyday life, and she'll never fight in the octagon again. In my opinion, those sacrifices she made for being in the public eye far exceed any obligation she may have had for being halfway famous."

David sat upright and buckled his seat belt. "However, our phones ring constantly with demands, and for her to find her new normal, she needs to put all of this behind her. I was outvoted about doing the interview this soon, and I've been Bear Hug's manager for two years now. I forgot how tough losing is. I shouldn't have taken that out on you."

As they merged back into traffic, Mack swallowed to relieve the tightness in his throat. It didn't work, so he cleared it before speaking. "What do you mean 'never fight in the octagon again'?"

David stiffened and adjusted his grip on the steering wheel. "That wreck ended her career."

Mack coughed and settled deeper into his seat. "Is she—is she paralyzed?" He'd feared that outcome since she disappeared, and he needed to know now so he didn't cry when he saw her. He didn't want to make a bad situation worse for her.

"No!" David exclaimed, glancing at him before refocusing on the road. "No. When she found out that one bad hit could be fatal, she realized a championship wasn't as important to her."

The injury must have been to her back or spine, Mack figured. He'd heard of football players who'd been in really bad wrecks having to retire due to spinal injuries because one bad hit would paralyze or kill them. Honestly, he agreed with her decision. Losing someone as kind and compassionate as Hazel Metcalf would be a true tragedy, and nothing mattered more than keeping that light in the world.

The rest of the drive passed in silence. All of the trees hung low with snow, and the mountaintops appeared hazy in the distance. Colorado blinded him, the sunlight reflecting off the snow in every direction. In his hurry this morning, he hadn't grabbed his sunglasses. However, he liked the change from the desert and neon of Vegas. Lots of natural beauty here. It'd be even better if it weren't covered in snow.

They turned on a narrow road with mounds of snow piled high on either side. If another vehicle met them, one of them would have to reverse, because there would be no passing. "We're the only cabin back here. Hazel's trainer, Vincent, owns this piece of property. It's just over fifty acres." He snorted and grinned. "The man likes his privacy."

Mack smiled. "His nearest neighbors are moose and deer and sheep. Probably pretty quiet."

"Coyotes, mountain lions, wolves, and bears, too. Don't travel far from the cabin by yourself. Even if you don't get lost or mauled to death, you could get trampled by territorial bison. This area is dangerous to tourists."

Mack watched the passing landscape more closely. "Trampled and mauled have both been added to the list of ways I don't want to die."

They followed the road around a curve, and a two-story cabin came into sight ahead. Smoke rolled out of the chimney, creating a picture-perfect scene. A long line of evergreen trees started to the left of the property and continued out the right, a small forest against a carpet of white. Mountains rose up in the distance, adding height to an otherwise flat land. Honestly, it deserved to grace the front of a Christmas card or something.

A truck was backed into a cleared spot ahead of them. A snowplow mounted on the front undoubtedly meant that the city did not clear private properties here. A wide shovel leaned up against the wall beside the front door, explaining the path from the parking area to the front door. David glanced at him as he shut the engine off, somehow more serious now that they'd arrived. "Kick the snow off your shoes on the porch step, take your shoes off inside the cabin, and don't forget that it's a long, freezing walk back to the airport."

Mack grabbed his jacket and briefcase from the back seat and stepped out. He was relieved when he thought back to the socks he'd put on that morning. This pair didn't have any holes, and they were actually clean.

Before he could get to the back of the SUV, David had his

suitcase out of the hatch and had started to walk toward the front door. He literally kicked the front of each shoe against the step's riser as he walked up the stairs. Mack followed the example.

Just before David reached it, the front door opened. Mack glimpsed Hazel's face briefly before she stepped behind the wooden door to let them through. David was unlacing his boots to the right of the doorway. He stepped in, toeing off his tennis shoes as she shut the door. He smiled at her as he bent over to move the shoes to the line of diverse footwear on a mat, presumably intended to catch the water as the snow melted off them.

"Welcome to Colorado, Mack," she murmured, her hands hidden beneath the fleece shawl she wore. "Thank you so much for taking the time to meet us."

"I appreciate you offering me this opportunity."

He caught her glaring over his shoulder, but by the time he glanced back, David stood with a neutral expression while holding his suitcase. "Mack, I believe David is going to show you to your room and let you settle in. I'm going to make some hot tea. Would you like some?"

He hesitated, and David added, "There's probably coffee in the pot too."

Mack nodded, grateful for the save. "Coffee will be great."

Hazel smiled at him and headed toward the kitchen. She bumped her shoulder against David's as she passed, causing her manager to grin like he'd been caught misbehaving but hadn't gotten scolded. When he looked at Mack, his expression moved closer to his normal frown.

He followed David down the hallway. "Bathroom. Washer and dryer are in there if you need them. That's a storage closet if you need a towel. This is your room. Upstairs is off-limits, as is the room across the hall. Please stick to the living area, kitchen, bathroom, and your bedroom for the privacy of the others."

David set his suitcase down with a thunk, and Mack hesitated in the hallway. "Do you need anything?" David asked, obviously reluctant.

"When my boss said I'd be staying in a cabin..."

"He meant you were staying in our cabin, yes."

Mack nodded slowly, processing the thought. "And—off the record, of course—are you and Hazel dating?"

David's frown turned to a scowl. "No. She is like a sister to me. That means her mental and physical health are important to me. She has a lot going on right now, and she doesn't need to be dating anyone. Understood?"

Feeling trapped, Mack agreed quickly. "Yessir." He stepped against the wall as David passed him and headed back down the hallway and up the stairs.

He sighed once he heard the floor creaking overhead, unsure why the other man intimidated him this badly. Mack often interviewed men physically larger than himself and much stronger. All of the male MMA fighters could lift him over their heads, and some of the females could too. Something about the air around David Gonzalez felt strong and scary, like he had a hidden dimension just wanting to come out and break him in half.

He set the suitcase on the edge of the bed, which was piled high with comforters. Most of the clothes, he hung up to try to de-wrinkle. A small table and overstuffed chair in the corner were his best options for a desk, though his overflow could go to the top of the chest of drawers. Using the top drawer, he put his boxers and socks all together. Then he zipped the empty suitcase and put it under the bed.

Lifting up the curtain and looking out the window, he spotted a large shed about thirty yards from the cabin. Someone had shoveled out the front of it. Snowshoe-shaped footprints led to it, and two ski-looking tracks appeared to have left it and headed toward the trees.

Soft footsteps came down the hallway, and he walked back to the door to see Hazel approaching. She offered him a coffee mug, holding her own cup close to her chest. "Thank you."

She smiled. "It's the least I could do. I tried to convince the guys to let me ride along, but they didn't want me to spend that much time trapped in a vehicle. I promise, David was the best option of the three of them. Barry isn't much of a talker, and Vin is a little gruff with strangers. That's why David is in charge of public relations."

Mack's lips twitched. "He seemed more personable in front of a dozen reporters than when I was locked in an SUV with him. But he really cares about you, and I don't blame him for his concern. You all don't know me, and you're literally bringing me into your home during a stressful time. I don't hold it against him, and you shouldn't either."

Her shoulder rose and fell, and her smile turned mischievous. "I have to give him a hard time. He's an only child, and he needs someone to keep him grounded."

"He also says you tire quickly. Maybe we should go to the kitchen or living room where you can sit," Mack suggested, sipping the coffee. The bitter brew could use a dash of cream, but he'd drank much worse while on deadline. And it was hot. Just looking at the snow outside left him feeling chilled.

Hazel winced. "David worries too much, but the living room is more comfortable. I love sitting in front of the fireplace."

"Then lead the way."

He followed behind her, noticing the fuzzy house shoes and men's flannel pants beneath her long shawl. She looked comfortable and relaxed, not like someone who'd just lost her career. She'd trained and battled her way almost to the top, and some madman had stolen the chance for her to prove she was the best before she could hold the bantamweight belt above her head in the center ring. If it were him, he'd have a lot of resentment.

She chose the overstuffed chair closest the fire, pulling her feet out of the house shoes and tucking them under her. The tea balanced in one hand, she pulled the throw hanging over the back down to cover her lap and feet. After a few seconds of fiddling, she glanced up bashfully. "Sorry. I should have asked if you wanted this seat. Do you?"

He shook his head quickly. "I haven't been here long enough to have a preference, and you look too comfortable to move. Besides, I probably wouldn't be able to tell the difference between this chair and that one," he admitted as he sat in the one across from her.

She rested her head against the wing of the chair, staring into the fire as she sipped her tea. He watched her a long moment before realizing how rude he was being. Adjusting his attention to his cup of coffee, he also took a drink. "How are you doing, Hazel?"

Her grin as she peeked at him brightened the room, and he couldn't help but smile back.

"Sometimes I forget that the accident ever happened. Like right now, I feel like Vin gave me a rest day before pitting me against Barry tomorrow for a sparring match. A day of relaxation so sore muscles can mend. And I will train tomorrow, but it won't be for the next match or the championship. It'll be to make progress toward different goals, like bettering my control."

He nodded, hearing the resignation in her voice. "Can I watch?"

She set her tea mug on her knee. "Have you ever run wearing snowshoes?"

Raising his eyebrows, he shook his head. "I've never even walked in them."

"I don't imagine living in Vegas gives you many chances," she reassured. "Perhaps you should get some practice walking before you run. I don't think Barry will want to carry us both back."

His mouth pressed together at the thought of her needing that kind of help. "Does that happen often?"

Some of the light in her eyes dimmed. "Too often. I may not seem like it, but I'm quite stubborn and, in some arenas, competitive—especially with the guys. Sibling rivalry. Plus, I don't want to disappoint them. Sometimes I push myself beyond my new boundaries."

In the distance, a vehicle approached, higher pitched than a car or truck's engine. As it came closer, he noticed that the loud noise was actually two separate sounds. Realizing their time alone was coming to an end, he scooted forward slightly on the chair.

"Hazel, I'm a stranger and I don't know you guys well, but the man I rode with from the airport would never be disappointed in you. He's worried about you, protective of you, and proud of the person you are."

At the top of the stairs, David grunted. "The reporter is right, Hazelbear. I'm damned proud of you." He took the stairs two at a time and headed to the door to put on his boots. "Vin and Barry are back. You stay in here. I'll get the groceries."

Putting on his jacket and gloves, David stepped out on the porch and closed the door behind him. Through the window behind the couch, Mack saw two machines idling near the walkway, the skis under them explaining the tracks he'd seen from the shed. Two men bundled against the cold, wearing ski masks and goggles so that he couldn't tell which one was

36 | THIA MACKIN

Vin or Barry, unstrapped baskets and passed them to David to set on the porch.

"It takes almost forty minutes off the trip to the grocery on the snowmobiles versus the truck," Hazel explained softly, also watching out the door. "They take a straighter path, and we have permission from the neighbor to cut across his land." She grinned suddenly. "His wife likes me, which ended the tiny war he and Vin had engaged in for over a decade."

She unfurled her legs, sliding her feet back into the house shoes and draping the blanket over the back again. Then she set her tea on the small table beside the chair. "Be right back."

Opening the door as David carried the first bin inside, she took it from him to keep him from tracking snow beyond the doorway. The two snowmobiles started, the sound of the engines headed toward the shed. Mack stood, setting his own drink beside hers. Then he hurried to grab the next load from David. David nodded to him and shut the door to keep in the heat as he stepped outside.

Mack passed Hazel in the doorway, and she touched his shoulder gently. "Guests shouldn't do chores."

He paused a half-step before continuing on to set his bin beside hers. As he passed her again, he said, "I'm hoping some of this food is meant to feed me. In which case, I should do my part."

Her smile hurried his steps. This time, when he reached the door, Vin and Barry were stripping their gear off on the porch. David handed him another box of food, and he wondered how they got that much on the snowmobiles as David followed him inside with his arms full. Hazel took the last of the groceries from her manager so he could take his boots back off, and David reached outside to accept the bulky jackets to hang up to dry.

As Mack stood in the kitchen, he asked Hazel how they fit all the groceries. "Vin special ordered these bins, and he built a rack on the back of the snowmobiles that can each hold four of them. Obviously, we don't have to worry about food thawing on the trip. In the summer, though, we have a cooler for the ATV."

Mack watched as she began separating the groceries, and he put his hands in his pockets, feeling useless. She shook her head. "Go on and meet Vin and Barry. Barry does most of the cooking, and he's particular about where everything goes. Otherwise, I'd put you to work earning your keep." Her wink warmed him, and he tucked his head slightly in embarrassment before heading to the living area.

The men were stripped to their jeans and long-sleeved shirts, both standing by the fire warming themselves as David whispered to them. He hesitated, not sure if he should interrupt. However, Barry glanced at him, and the other two followed suit.

"Mack Godram," he introduced himself, meeting the younger of the two new arrivals halfway.

"Barry Litgram, physical therapist and bodyguard."

Mack shook his hand. "And chef, I hear."

Barry shook his head, glancing toward the kitchen. "It wouldn't be bad if one of us wasn't a vegetarian," he stated in a raised voice.

"More meat for the rest of you," Hazel cheerfully shouted from the kitchen, causing everyone to smile.

Mack interjected, "I'm not picky. Half of my meals come from the office vending machine, and the other half are usually from venues' concession stands."

Vin interrupted, his voice and demeanor gruff. "Glad you're here so we can get this over with. Hazel deserves some peace and quiet, and hopefully, your article will get that for her. I've got some work to do upstairs, but I'll see you at dinner. We can schedule your interview times then around her training."

38 | THIA MACKIN

With a quick nod, Vin turned on his heel and headed up the stairs.

"Ignore him," Hazel shouted from the kitchen. "I can't afford to pay him enough to be polite."

On the stairs, Vin snorted before continuing on up. Barry and David muttered at the same time, "Always poking the bear." The fondness on their faces, though, said more than the words.

After a long moment, Barry rolled his shoulder. "I'm going to take a hot shower and defrost. There's lunch meat if you want a snack, but leave the salad for Hazel. They don't have a lot of fresh greens at the small market this time of year. We'll have vegetables with supper, though."

David followed Barry upstairs, talking low but intently to him. Mack tried to listen in, but he could only catch the general sounds and no actual syllables. After a second, he moved toward the kitchen. Hazel had already set a plate and the sandwich fixings on the counter, and she was tossing salad in a container when he walked in.

"Help yourself!"

He glanced from the turkey and ham to her and back. "It won't offend you if I eat meat in front of you?"

She continued to shake her salad. "It's a personal choice for me, and I don't hold it against anyone else. In fact, I encountered a flock of wild turkey last week who nearly changed my stance on whether eating birds was okay. The tom—the male turkey—took offense to my entire existence, and he nearly caught me before I could run away."

Mack's eyes widened as he opened the loaf of bread. "I'm glad you escaped. It sounds harrowing. Were you on the snowmobile?"

Hazel set her salad on the table and held up a finger indicating she needed a minute before going toward the living room. When she returned, she set his coffee on the table and

BEAR HUG | 39

put her tea down beside the salad. "Barry and I were running. Only he laughed so hard he fell over, and the turkey found me the bigger threat."

Setting his plate on the table, he sat down across from her. "Obviously, he'd seen you fight."

She chewed her first bite and pointed her fork toward him. "You're sweet. He'd just never seen the guys tear into a chuck roast or turkey breast. If he had, he would have taken his little harem and run away."

The rest of their meal passed in silence. When she finished, Hazel washed both her cup and bowl then placed them in the drainer. "I'm going to take a nap, but if you need anything, knock on my door or yell for one of the guys. There are books on the shelf in the living room, and we have satellite for internet. There's a cable beside the couch if the wireless network acts up."

Mack nodded. "My morning started early. I'll actually probably take a nap myself. Thank you."

He washed his bowl and cup then followed her down the hallway. At the closed bedroom door, she grinned at him and waved before going inside and shutting it behind her. He didn't get a good look at the inside of the room, which left him oddly disappointed. After a moment, he stopped at the bathroom before going into his guest room. Shutting the door behind him, he made a few notes on his legal pad, closed the curtains to block the light, and crawled under the covers.

Closing his eyes, he tried to forget how warm Hazel's grin and wave made him. Hopefully, they could do the interview tomorrow and he could be on his way. With her three protectors hovering overhead, he'd have his ass handed to him if he looked at her sideways.

CHAPTER 4

"You really think I can't take care of myself?" Hazel asked, her voice full of hurt.

She looked up at Barry, her eyes misty. She reminded herself not to tighten her grip on the kitchen doorframe. As an Ursus, her strength far surpassed what she'd had as a human. The past two months as she'd adjusted, she'd broken two mugs—including her favorite one—and crushed a door handle by pulling before she'd fully turned it.

"Hazelbear, don't you look at me like that," he growled, running his hand over his face before looking directly in her eyes. "You know that I'd bet on you in a fight every single time, against any comers. But that's not what this is about." He jerked his thumb in the general direction of the guest bedroom. "That reporter definitely isn't going to physically fight you."

Relieved, she relaxed. Her lips twitched, and the hurt left her eyes. She lowered her voice, batted her eyelashes, and mock-whispered, "Do you think he might… kiss me?"

Barry's eyes widened then narrowed. "You are *not* funny. A million things could happen in twenty-four hours. Like"—

he grasped mentally for the worst thing he could think of—"an avalanche!"

She couldn't help it. Cocking her hip and raising her brow, she slowly blinked at him. "And you think you and David and Vin could stop an avalanche?" She looked up toward the ceiling where Vin was grumbling quietly, just loud enough for her paranormal hearing to pick up the cadence but not hear the words. "Really, an avalanche?"

He grinned ruefully. "Maybe not. It's just that this is all still new to you, and I wish this audience happened when you could go with us too. Not when you have company."

Hazel honestly wished she could go also. The Eiffel Creek Lykos pack territory began about ten miles away, and the leader had offered their four-person arktoi sanctuary inside their town. The story Paolo had told her this morning on the phone had sounded surreal, way crazier than humans who turned into bears or wolves.

Hundreds of years ago, a powerful witch named Angelia Cunningham had given her life trying to protect a Lykos pack who'd lived peacefully in her woods. Unfortunately, she witnessed most of the pack murdered by the humans on a witch hunt before they drowned her. In her final moments, she'd unleashed a blessing. Her spirit would forever link with the khan of the pack, hiding and protecting the remaining members. Typically, the monarch of a therianthrope species assigned the nobility, excepting the Eiffel Creek pack. Angelia—whom they called their angel—chose and bonded with the person in charge of them. And this interview would determine whether the pack would allow a small group of bears to live in their town.

She patted Barry's arm. "Just turn on your charm. It'll be nice not having to share a house with you lot all the time and living somewhere I don't have to worry constantly that I'll somehow ruin everyone's lives."

"You could never ruin anyone's life. You're our *blessing*, Hazelbear." Barry kissed her cheek, and she beamed at him. He sighed, defeated. "Go for a walk if you need to let off steam, yeah?"

"Bear-ly anything to worry about," she joked, waving her fingers at him. "Don't keep them waiting. We can't make a bad first impression."

He narrowed his eyes at her. "Remember, cell phones don't work well there. If we don't answer, try the landline on the fridge if there's an emergency. The man who answers—Buchanan Rafferty—can get a message to us. If they decide we can't stay, we'll be back tonight. Otherwise, we'll be back tomorrow after we've found houses for us to live."

Footsteps approached, and they both waited until David popped in to make sure it wasn't their guest. "I'm excited. We hear occasional whispers about the secret Lykos pack, but to actually *see* them?" David rolled his eyes back until only the white showed and gestured in excitement.

"I didn't realize I was taking a couple toddlers with me. Maybe you two should stay here and Hazel go with me," Vin groused.

David shrugged. "They'd definitely like her better than us. I'm okay with this. I can entertain the journalist."

The timer went off, and Barry pulled the skewers out to set on the serving tray with the oven mitts. Then he took a couple vegetable-only ones to put inside. "Don't forget..."

"Protein shake with dinner," she finished for him.

"And make sure..." he started.

"I'll have mixed nuts for a snack before bed, and I'm going to make guac with the avocados you bought to go with lunch tomorrow. I'll be a good girl and finish all of my veggies. No candy. Promise."

He snorted. "There's no candy in this cabin."

BEAR HUG | 43

She laughed and hummed. "None that you know of," she continued in a singsong.

Vin came forward to one-arm hug her. "Stop taunting them. Behave. Be careful. If something happens, don't let him leave until we return to smooth it out."

"Uh-huh," she murmured, knowing no one in the room expected her to hold Mack Godram hostage. "I'll go for a run in the morning down the usual path. Just in case I'm not here when you come back, you'll know where to come dig me out if that worst-case scenario comes true and we have an avalanche."

Vin squeezed her again before accepting a couple of the meat-laden skewers from Barry and picking a couple pieces off with his fingers. "An avalanche, huh?" After he chewed the first bite, he nodded solemnly. "We might be due for one, because the last one was, well, never."

Barry used a fork to empty his skewers onto a plate and stabbed a combination of beef and peppers with the tines. "She put me on the spot. It was the worst thing I could think of at the time."

David also went the finger route, pulling pieces off and popping them directly in his mouth. "A stampede of bison, maybe. With that wild herd that took down the fence earlier in the year, that's a much more immediate concern."

Hazel opened the convection oven and turned the vegetable skewers. "I'll try not to spook the car-sized, shaggy dogs on the property."

Vin moved to the sink and ran dishwater into it. "Bison can take down a mountain lion. You'd need to be the size of a bear to possibly make them rethink their approach. Their weight alone can crush a person much bigger than you, not to mention what their horns can do." He finished washing his skewers and his cup. "You've lived here too long to be flippant about safety, Hazel. Don't make us find your body somewhere. We won't take it well."

She hugged him, ignoring his damp hands on her back. "I'll be careful, guys. You all watch yourselves too."

David hugged her when she stepped away from Vin. Then he washed his dishes and nudged her toward Barry where the process repeated again. The timer went off again, and Barry broke away to pull her vegetables out. Slipping them off the skewers and onto a plate, he handed it to her and nudged her to the table. Then he took the remaining skewers and emptied them into a Tupperware bowl to place in the microwave for Mack.

"Want company while you eat?" David asked.

She poured hot water from the electric kettle into her cup then pulled out the ingredients to make her protein shake. As she mixed them in the blender, she waved idly at them. "You all go on. Honestly, a few minutes of alone time will be nice. I love you all, but we haven't had any real time apart since before the accident. It'll do us all good."

Vin patted both guys on the shoulder and ushered them out of the kitchen with goodbyes, I love yous, and be carefuls. She poured the protein shake in a tall glass, carrying both the tea and the shake to the table as David and Barry groused at each other. Finally, after a little scuffle by the door while they put on boots and coats, the door closed behind them. Outside the SUV started and idled a minute before the tires crunched on the snow. Sitting down and leaning her head back, she closed her eyes and exhaled softly.

"Want me to eat in my room?" Mack asked from the doorway, probably lured by the smell of food and the sounds of the blender.

Tensing, she straightened and then smiled. "I did not hear you come down the hallway. Sorry about that. Please join me."

BEAR HUG | 45

Hazel stood, heading to the microwave to pull out the Tupperware, a plate, and silverware. He didn't know where everything would be, and she didn't feel right just pointing from her chair. "There is a pitcher of water, a couple beers, and a few sodas in the fridge. I also have a huge assortment of teas. What would you like?"

"Please, I'll get it. You don't need to serve me." He opened the fridge and pulled out a soda after a brief hesitation.

Moving back to her seat, she tucked her head over her plate so he didn't feel like she stared. After a moment, the smell of seasoned beef and onions became strong. Then he settled across from her.

"How did you find your team?" Mack asked, going to take his first bite.

She grinned when his eyes lit up at the taste. People were always surprised at how well Barry cooked the first time they ate his meals. He could make vegetables taste heavenly, to the point where she rarely craved meat. Even now, she maintained her vegetarianism up until the three days of the full moon. She'd nearly bitten David's hand off for his steak last month—in her human form. Luckily, Vin said the aggressive need for meat would ease as time passed. Now going into her fourth full moon, she'd ward it off as much as possible.

"On or off the record?" she asked, not that the story changed much between the two. Mostly, she was curious whether or not he was making conversation or working.

He paused, fork halfway to his mouth, and considered. "Sorry. I forgot for a minute why you invited me here. I guess, on the record?"

Digging in his back pocket, he pulled out a small notepad and pen. Opening it to a blank page, he set it beside his right hand before picking his fork back up.

"Honestly, it's the same story either way." She sipped the shake, thinking back. "The original trainer I started with was

46 | THIA MACKIN

my then-boyfriend. He knew about a third of what an actual trainer needed to know, and he knew less than that about how a boyfriend should act. Vin found me upset outside the locker room the day I broke it off with the guy, whose name I do not want in a news article because he deserves none of the credit for what Vin accomplished with me."

Honestly, for a second, she couldn't remember the guy's name. Vin had nicknamed him Fumbles, and she'd never spoken his name after she'd caught him having sex with a random woman in the locker room that day.

"Vin took me to the far corner and peppered me with questions. When did I start martial arts? How many forms had I studied? Had I heard of mixed martial arts? By the time my ex had finished showering with his new girlfriend, I had a new trainer. As you can tell, I got the best end of that."

Mack chewed slowly, his eyes on her as she told the story. His pen remained on the table, and she felt confident enough to continue.

"I continued to work—I have my MBA and worked for a private company then—and train for about six months. Then Vin introduced me to David, who watched me spar with a couple of the other fighters at the gym. They decided I was ready to book an amateur fight. Within a couple days, he'd got me on the ticket for a reputable amateur women's fight. I won, but it wasn't pretty, and the money wasn't good. Vin identified some weaknesses for us to work on. Once he was satisfied, I went back into the octagon again. Second time went better. Third time better still. However, I tweaked my shoulder in training, which is when Vin suggested adding Barry to our circle."

Mack had scooted his empty plate away and nodded along with her story. "Barry is your physical therapist and your bodyguard?"

She nodded. "He is a licensed physical therapist, which

the Army paid for after he got out. While I could probably be my own bodyguard, just having someone Barry's size around stops a lot of issues before they begin. No matter how many fights I win, people don't find me intimidating. A six-foot-three former military man who carries himself like he could lift a truck? Keeps the crazy fans at a distance." Her face fell for a second. "Well, most of them."

Mack reached over and touched her hand. "Hey, we aren't talking about that now. Tell me more about your trio to success in the early days. When did they decide you were ready?"

She squeezed his hand gratefully. "They didn't. If you learn anything while you are here, it'll be that they are incredibly protective of me. We're a little family, and they are definitely classic older brothers. A representative from World Fighting Inc. saw me fight about a year into my amateur career. It was a seventeen-second technical knock-out. They caught us in the parking lot and offered me a contract."

Mack grinned. "And then it was on."

She held up her hand and shook her head. "Definitely not. David negotiated the contract for two months, and Vin nearly killed me in training. They were all scared it was too soon to put me in the octagon with bantamweight professionals. But finally, WFI put their foot down, and the match was on the bill."

"And *then* it was on?" he questioned, looking hopeful.

She looked up at the ceiling, remembering it. "I was a nervous wreck," she admitted, meeting his eyes. "A dozen strangers brought me roses, welcoming me to WFI's team. All of them told me there was no shame in losing my first professional fight, but I hadn't lost yet, and I didn't *want* to lose. It really got in my head, and nothing Vin or David said could knock me out of the funk. Then I bumped into this super-nice sports reporter in the hallway. He introduced himself, and he didn't act like a newcomer was destined to lose. Suddenly, everything felt back on track. And I walked into the ring, did my thing, and... *then* it was on."

Hazel grinned at him, reaching over to touch his hand a moment before pulling back. "So thank you for being part of my team that night. You kind of became my good luck charm. Each fight, people told me things like, 'A winning streak doesn't last forever. It's okay to lose.' And every fight, I proved them wrong with the guys in my corner and you waiting in the reporters' conference room." She nodded. "You were the first reporter I met, and I thought it would be appropriately full-circle to have you be the last to interview me."

His face fell, though he smiled for her. "It's been a pleasure. I am sorry that accident ended your career. You were definitely going to knock Michaela Quinn out."

For just a moment, Hazel's lower lip trembled. Then her eyes cleared, she took a long draw of her protein shake, and she shrugged a shoulder. "The good news is that I will always be undefeated in the ring, and we can forever say things like 'I would have definitely KO'd her in the first round' without ever being proven wrong."

Mack tilted his head, making her feel like a curious bird studied her. "Do you always find the bright side in everything?"

"Of course not," she argued. However, the hairs on her arms stood up like lightning was about to strike her down for the lie. "Fine. Strong possibility. But sometimes the optimism presents itself, and I don't have to do anything."

"You're a good person, Hazel."

The compliment made her uncomfortable, and she decided to take her dishes to the sink. Adding hot water into the dishwater Vin had run earlier, she cleaned her plate.

Mack's chair scooted back, and she inhaled the subtle scent of his cologne as he stood. Unlike many of the fragrances she'd sniffed at the store last week that burned her nose, his didn't overwhelmingly contain rubbing alcohol. Instead, it teased her senses.

"Anything I can do to help?" he asked.

His arm brushed hers as he set his plate and utensils on the counter, and she concentrated on rinsing the glass in her hand. *He's here to do a job. He isn't here for you to corner in a cabin in the middle of nowhere surrounded by three feet of snow.*

"Uh, Hazel, is my being alone with you here without your family making you uncomfortable?" He scuffed his shoe on the floor, stepping away from her. "I'm sorry. That's not my intent."

Blinking, Hazel turned off the water and set the glass in the drainer. A quiet giggle escaped her, and she looked around for the dish towel to dry her hands. "Mack, not even close."

He raised an eyebrow at her. "Because you could knock me to the floor in ten seconds or less?"

His expression challenged her, and dang, the predator in her rose to accept it. The powerful creature living under her skin stretched, not tearing or trying to push out through her skin. Just a subtle reminder of who she was now. "If I take you to the floor, we wouldn't be brawling, sweetheart."

For a second, shock flashed in his eyes before he set his hand on the counter and half-stepped toward her. "What *would* we be doing, Hazel?"

She raised her eyebrow at him in return and stepped forward, their heights similar enough that her nose nearly touched his. A deep breath filled her with another hint of his cologne. "This," she warned softly.

The last inch disappeared as she leaned toward him, a hand on his shoulder to steady herself. His lips were soft and warm beneath hers, not resisting as she gently kissed him. Pulling back, she peeked at him when he didn't kiss her back. He stood stock still, his eyes closed, before he blinked twice and looked at her.

His hazel eyes held warmth, and he touched his mouth cautiously with his fingers. "You should try that again. I wasn't ready the first time. Thought I might have dreamed it."

Sliding her hand over to the back of his neck, she tugged him into her. This time, his lips met hers eagerly. Tilting her head to better explore, she enjoyed the warmth of his arm wrapped around her back. His other hand brushed from her shoulder to elbow and back up.

Out of breath, she leaned back and grinned at him. He opened his eyes, brushing his fingers over her cheek. "Once more? I wasn't ready that time either," he whispered.

"Mmm. Maybe you'd expect it if we moved to the couch, closer to the fireplace?" she suggested playfully, linking her fingers with his and leading him to the living room.

When she stopped, he used his hand in hers to twirl her. The unexpected move caused her to giggle as he steadied her with his other hand on her hip. He wiggled his eyebrows at her. "Now who's caught off guard?"

She placed her palm on his chest and gently pushed him back toward the couch. "I'll have you know, I'm trained to expect the unexpected. I just needed to test your reactions."

He settled back onto the couch, lifting his chin. "Oh, a feint to the left to check my moves?"

Climbing onto the couch, she straddled his lap with one hand on each shoulder. "I'm *definitely* interested in your moves, Mack. Show me what you've got."

Shrugging her shoulders, she allowed the shawl to fall to the floor behind her. The cool air raised goosebumps on her arms, and his hands started at her tank top straps and trailed

BEAR HUG | 51

to her elbow and back up to warm her skin. The gentle touches caused her to shiver. As she leaned forward, he gripped the back of her neck and slowly pulled her closer as his gaze met hers. The corner of her mouth lifted, and she leaned forward to erase the distance.

Just before her lips touched his, she inhaled the musky scent of his cologne and closed her eyes. Her fingers rested on his shoulders, careful not to accidentally tighten down and hurt him with her paranormal strength. Instead, she concentrated on the movement of his mouth over hers, the warmth spreading out from their points of contact.

His lips tugged at hers, and she opened to his gentle exploration. He tasted of sugar and warmth, things she craved almost as much as she wanted him. She sighed as he pulled back, moving his hand from her neck to brush his thumb over the blush in her cheeks. After a moment, she slipped off his lap and cuddled her chest up to his side. Resting her head against his shoulder, Hazel pressed her lips to his neck. "You seem like a worthy adversary."

He chuckled, running his knuckles up then down her spine. "Admittedly, I had a couple rounds to study your moves. A little practice helped me keep up."

Hazel smiled softly. Just touching Mack brought her a peace she hadn't felt in months, not since training for that last fight had put her in the quiet place where fear and doubt and negativity didn't live. She adored her arktoi, but they bickered like siblings. The only time they were silent for more than five minutes was when Vin told them to shut up or when they were running in bear form. This man, though, didn't feel the need to pepper the moment with small talk.

The fire popped, and Hazel realized she should check it. If it went out, she'd have to fight to start it back up or they would freeze. The small heaters in the other rooms only worked in conjunction with the warmth put off by the large fireplace or if the door to the room was closed to keep all of the heat inside. Mornings were miserable for the first hour.

"Hazel," Mack murmured hesitantly, his hand finding and squeezing hers lightly as he straightened. She also sat upright and pressed her thumb into his palm in acknowledgement, careful not to clutch his in return. "I-I'm sorry. This crosses the line for journalistic integrity. I should not kiss someone I'm doing an article on."

For a moment, all Hazel heard was his rejection. She reached down and grabbed her shawl, carefully wrapping it back around her shoulders. The movement allowed her time to think, and she realized he was right. If they began a relationship during her article, it might call into question the truth of what he wrote. And more than anything, she and her family needed his words to put her career to rest. The dozens of phone calls a day requesting interviews, television appearances, and updates exhausted all of them.

Plus, what would it do to Mack's career if his integrity was questioned?

She moved to the fireplace, adding two pieces of wood carefully. "I should apologize too. After asking you to come here, the least I could do is allow you to do your job without interference."

He grinned, coming up behind her and using his socked foot to nudge her leg. "Honestly, that was the best 'interference' I've ever experienced. To be clear, the only thing I'm sorry about is that I can't kiss you again."

The ache in her chest eased, and she turned to face Mack with a soft smile of invitation. "Maybe one day after you submit your article, you can return to Colorado to see how you feel about ski slopes, hiking in the snow, and recently retired MMA fighters?"

He reached out and took her hand. "I do have some vacation days available. Once the article comes out, you can decide if you're still interested in hiking with a somewhat out of shape sports journalist."

She laughed. "Deal." Shaking her head, she gently pulled her hand free. "For now, I'll excuse myself. I'm going to go soak in the tub and read a bit. The house is never this quiet, and I should take advantage of it before the noisy trio returns tomorrow."

Hazel checked the locks on the windows and doors before making herself a cup of tea and turning off the coffee pot in the kitchen. She remembered her promise and grabbed the can of mixed nuts for a snack. After a deep breath, she stepped out and headed toward her room.

"Mack, be sure to turn the heater on in your room and shut your door when you go to bed. Otherwise, you'll freeze in the morning. I'll come back out and bank the fire in a few hours, so don't worry about it. And help yourself to whatever snacks you want."

"Goodnight, Hazel."

"Sleep well, Mack."

Just before she entered her room, she looked over her shoulder to see him sitting on the couch with his head in his hands.

Me too, buddy. Me too.

CHAPTER 5

Mack woke up to light pouring in the window. Pulling the cover over his head, he vaguely remembered opening the curtains last night to realize no moon could be found in the sky. Then he'd made notes from his conversation with Hazel about her beginning in the industry and wrote a reminder to ask her trainer what he'd seen in the amateur fighter. When he crawled into bed, he couldn't stop thinking about Hazel kissing him. About how he had never wanted her to stop.

Blindly reaching out to the nightstand, he felt for his watch or cell phone. Finally, his fingers grabbed his watch band and pulled it beneath the comforter. Only, he couldn't read it. Sighing, he lifted the corner to let in enough light to read the face.

6:59 A.M.

He groaned. His normal day didn't start until at least eight, but these past two days of waking early were worth it. He was in Colorado interviewing Hazel "Bear Hug" Metcalf for the final article of her career. And telling this gorgeous, kind, compassionate, and basically perfect woman that he couldn't kiss her while alone in a cabin in the woods because he needed to remain unbiased damn near killed him.

A disbelieving snort escaped him, and he pulled the topmost cover under his chin.

He hadn't been unbiased about Hazel since two seconds after they bumped into one another that arena hallway. From the moment he met her eyes and she smiled, he'd essentially stepped into her corner as an invisible member of her team. However, as stupid as it felt and as unhappy as it made him, he'd done the right thing last night.

Climbing out of bed, he shivered at the chill in the air. He dressed quickly and pulled on his best pair of socks before going to the bathroom to complete his morning routine. Refreshed, he took his shaving kit back to his room before heading toward the kitchen and the smell of coffee.

Hazel smiled as he entered and wished her a good morning. She drank the last of what appeared to be another protein shake. Bundled against the cold, she seemed comfortable and wide awake. "There is leftover bacon, sausage, and biscuits from the guys' breakfast yesterday in the two blue Tupperware bowls. There are also fruit cups, oatmeal, or meal-replacement shakes."

He only hesitated a moment before pulling out the Tupperware from the fridge. She'd already set a mug, plate, and silverware out on the counter for him. He loaded the plate down and popped it in the microwave before putting the containers away and fixing a cup of the coffee. He'd spied sugar and creamer last night while hunting for snacks and doctored it to the perfect color.

Leaning against the counter, he took a careful sip. "How long have you been awake?"

She grinned. "Vin didn't turn off his alarms, which start going off every morning at five-thirty. I'm almost certain he left them active on purpose, knowing I'd have to go upstairs to turn them off, which would get my blood pumping enough I wouldn't be able to go back to sleep." Lowering her voice, she looked behind her as though making sure he wasn't listening. "He's sneakier than he looks."

"Well, he already looks pretty sneaky." The microwave timer went off behind him, and he set his mug on the table before carrying his plate over. After sitting, he took another sip of the coffee, hoping the caffeine helped him wake up. Then he picked up the biscuit and immediately dropped it again as it burned his fingers. "Shit. Sorry!"

She waved away his apology. "I've already shoveled the walkways, and I'll head out on my hike in about an hour. The sun makes a lot of difference in how cold it feels. But once you finish eating, we can go over more of your questions."

Mack grabbed a couple napkins from the stack in the middle of the table. "Let me make my sausage biscuit, and I'll multitask."

He pulled the small spiral notepad, a pen, and a folded sheet of paper out of his pocket before tearing the now-cooled biscuits in half and making two sandwiches. He took a quick bite and read over his list of questions. "Who coined the term 'Bear Hug'?"

Hazel pursed her lips, thinking. "I-I'm not sure, actually. Wow! That's a good question. I remember hearing it at the press conference for my second professional fight, I think."

She stared over his shoulder in thought, and he glanced back down at his notes. "The first time I heard it used as your nickname was your third fight against Natalie Garcia. The announcer said something like 'Will Hazel 'Bear Hug' Metcalf be able to grapple Natalie 'The Fist' Garcia into submission before it's lights out?' And I thought that man hadn't seen a single one of your fights, because both of your matches had ended in TKOs, not tap outs. What does grappling have to do with technical knockouts?"

Hazel chuckled. "Nothing, but the announcers are paid to hype the crowd." She set her empty cup down and leaned forward. "I'm going to hypothesize, but you should maybe do a follow-up with David. Heaven knows that man paid a lot more attention to the media coverage of my fights than I ever did. The guys call me Hazelbear, and as often as they do, it is entirely possible someone overheard the nickname. My first match, the bell ended the first round before I could make Nadia Bandy tap out. I had her grappled in a submission hold that Vin calls Total Tap Out that kind of looks like a very aggressive reverse hug, and she was literally seconds from tapping when the bell saved her."

He nodded, scribbling notes. "You came out of your corner like a hurricane second round. Two solid punches and she hit the floor. No—what did you say Vin calls it?—dancing and weaving?"

"Duck and weave! Move your feet!" Hazel growled gruffly. "Oh yeah. He'd pointed out this mistake I made—I don't even remember what I'd done—and it really hyped me up. She'd gotten in a couple really good jabs, and I had this thought that that one little mistake meant my entire left side would be a bruised mess. So I stepped on the mat frustrated with myself, and it gave me this moment of hyperfocus where I noticed that she kept dropping her left hand. I took the opening, and she took a nap." She held up a hand. "I never recommend losing your temper in a fight. Just ask Barry how often he's kicked my butt after taunting me. However, a little introspection sometimes opens a whole new perspective."

"What was your favorite fight?" he asked, still scribbling notes.

Hazel hummed. "Umm... each one taught me something about the industry and about myself. I was *really* looking forward to pitting myself against Michaela Quinn. I've studied all of her fights, practiced against her strengths, and trained against her weaknesses. I've never officially met her, but she became another—albeit invisible—member of the team. Now I don't ever get to test myself against her, never get to find out if what we did would be enough to elevate me to bantamweight champion."

He paused in his writing to glance at her. "How did someone as nice as you decide to pursue a career punching people in the face?"

Her eyes sparkled. "You do what you're good at, right?" Her laugh warmed the air, quite a feat with the amount of snow he saw outside the window. "Honestly, though, it started when my parents put me in karate. Age five, I remember asking Dad on the way home from the dojo why the only noise I could hear on the mats was sensei's voice. I don't remember his answer, but I can still see him looking at me through the rearview mirror and grinning with pride. By the time I was eight or nine, I had lessons in taekwondo, karate, and jiu jitsu five nights a week."

She picked up her empty cup and then set it back down. Leaning back, she pulled her shawl closer. "Dad was killed in an accident at the factory where he worked when I was in seventh grade. Mom continued taking me to practice, because she knew he'd have wanted that. And more than ever, I needed that silence I found on the mats. No wondering if I could have kept him home from work that day or made him late so he wasn't the person called to handle the machine malfunction."

Her sad smile pulled at his heart, and he wanted to reach over to hold her hand as she continued. "Right after we lost him, I convinced Mom to take self-defense classes, but she found her quiet place in running. She would wake up at Vino'clock and do ten miles. She said the vibrations as her feet hit the pavement grounded her. Bone cancer took her my sophomore year of college."

"I'm sorry," he murmured, not sure what else to say.

"No, I'm sorry. I went off-topic," she sniffled and pulled her shawl closer. "You asked why I fight. From bell ring to bell ring, all the noise falls away. The vibrations through the floor of the octagon, the impact of a jab connecting, the pop of a kick landing, the tremors of our muscles as an opponent fights a hold—they are this silent language where I have to concentrate on not harming the person in the ring with me."

"Punching someone in the face isn't harming them?" Mack asked, his lips twitching.

She leaned forward, intent. "A punch to the face hurts someone. An illegal hold that might break a joint or a bite that can cause infection and muscle or nerve damage harms them. We walk into the ring expecting to get hurt, but we trust each other not to cause harm. Can someone struggle in a legal hold instead of tapping and dislocate their own shoulder? Yes. But that isn't the fault of the person doing the hold. We train on how we can and cannot escape those grapples. We know the risks. It lets me forget the hate crimes, the terrorist attacks, and the meanness in the world for seconds or minutes inside that octagon where the only thing important is that my opponent and I follow these strict rules by listening to this unusual language that only she and I are speaking."

Mack swallowed, uncertain how to follow up. He hadn't expected her answer, so he took extra time to make sure his notes were clear. She scooted her chair back, taking her cup to the sink to wash it. Then she put the kettle on and pulled a mug out of the cabinet for tea. She turned back to him as she waited for the kettle to boil.

He set his pen down and finished eating, cleaning his plate despite the ball of lead sitting in his stomach. Finally, Mack stood too. His voice croaked on the beginning of the question, but he had to ask. "Hazel, where will you find your quiet now?"

For a long moment, she looked at the floor. The teakettle whistled, and she moved back to the stove to pour the boiling water over the tea bag. She glanced over her shoulder and raised it in a sad shrug.

"I don't know."

She sighed, gripped the mug by the handle, and headed to the living room. Not wanting to interrupt, he stayed in the kitchen to clean up his mess.

MACK GLANCED AT HIS WATCH AGAIN. TWO HOURS AND FIVE minutes since Hazel left for her hike. He knew the exact time she left, because she wrote it in the top corner of a dry-erase board on the fridge, and he'd looked at it at least five times in the past hour.

How long could she be out in the snow before hypothermia set in? Resolved, he headed for his bedroom to get his laptop and look it up. As he stepped into the hallway, a phone rang behind him. An older style phone sat on a table near the staircase, and it rang a third time before he changed direction to answer it.

"Uh, Diaz residence?" he tried, remembering that Vin owned the home.

"Is this Mack?" a confused, male voice asked. "Where's Hazel?"

Mack concentrated on the voice, trying to identify which of the team it was. "Is this Barry? Yes, this is Mack! And Hazel went on a hike over two hours ago but hasn't returned."

Barry cursed. "Are you sure of the time? Minutes can feel like hours."

Mack snorted. "Oh, I'm sure. She wrote it on the board in the kitchen."

"Hold on." In the background, he heard Barry talking to someone. Then he was back. "Okay. If she followed procedure, which it sounds like she intended to since she wrote down the time, she should have returned an hour and a half after she left. It'll take you about thirty minutes to gear up. If you put everything on and she comes back, great. Tell her that her family overreacted and sent you out. She'll be mad at us instead of you."

Mack nodded, not caring that Barry couldn't see him, impatient for the instructions to end so he could go look for her.

His new trainer wasn't anywhere near finished, though. "Do you know how to drive a snowmobile?"

"I might be able to figure it out," Mack tried.

"No. No, you might topple it over on you. Go on foot. The main path she took is marked with poles painted yellow going away from the house and marked green coming back to the house. Do not venture away from the poles; do not follow any other colors. If you do, you'll never find your way back to the cabin."

"Got it," Mack agreed, pulling the phone away from his ear for a second to see if anyone was visible out the window. Nothing moved.

"We all keep a spare set of boots by the door, so find the pair that fits best. Use the extra gear hanging on the wall. Mittens are better to prevent frostbite than gloves. Make sure you take poles to keep your balance if you go for snowshoes—which you should. There is a first aid kit under the couch that contains a number of heating patches. Strap it to your back. You don't want to drop it in a drift, and you'll make better time if you can use your hands."

David's voice came through the line, obviously standing

close to the receiver. "Mack, if you find yourself tiring, come back. You won't help anyone if you end up needing rescue too. Do you understand?"

Before Mack could tell him to fuck off, Barry said, "Vin has the SUV pulled around. We would normally be an hour away, but we'll be there in less time. I'll try to reach the neighbors with snowmobiles. If she comes back or if you find her, have her call our cell phones until someone picks up. We're on our way."

The line disconnected, and Mack ran for his bedroom to grab extra pairs of socks and warmer clothes. Adding layers quickly, he then headed for the couch to get the first aid kit. The kit was already set up in a backpack, like they expected problems to happen outside the cabin. Dropping it by the door, he began checking the shoes for sizes, impatiently pulling the tongues out to scan them. Someone was a half-size bigger than him, and he set those by the backpack before pulling the closest snowsuit off the hook to check the size.

"Nope," he growled, tossing what had to be Barry's back on the hook. He'd have at least a foot of extra material in the leg. The man was a giant. The next one, though, was sized correctly and looked like it would fit. Pulling it on, he zipped it up before realizing he'd need to unzip it again to put on his boots. "I hate the snow. This is ridiculous." He pulled his arms back out of the suit, almost winding himself while fighting the gear.

No wonder Hazel had wanted him to practice walking in snowshoes before accompanying her and David had sounded worried about him going out. He did cardio and made multiple gym visits a week. He shouldn't be out of breath from putting on clothes, he thought as he carefully buckled the snowshoes to his boots. This time, Mack waited until he finished putting on the gaiter, goggles, and secured the snowsuit hood before zipping the suit back up. Then he shrugged on the backpack and slipped on the gloves with mitten-like attachments. Grabbing the pair of adjustable poles, he glanced at the clock.

It took him just over thirty minutes to find everything and suit up. Now Hazel was well and truly late. With a deep breath, he opened the door and stepped out onto the porch, nearly pitching forward onto his face as his snowshoes touched and tangled.

I need a wider stance, he noted as he closed the door. Trying another step successfully, Mack walked carefully down the stairs and scanned for the path. Luckily, Hazel's tracks were still visible. No new snow had fallen, and the wind hadn't blown old snow over the trail. Mack reminded himself to walk slowly and carefully as he spotted the first yellow-painted pole. As David had warned, a stupid mistake on his part would only worsen things.

He stayed on the path as it entered the wooded area, noticing as he searched for clues that her snowshoe prints looked different than his. Also, her stride was wider, like she'd run the path.

Was she Superwoman? Rocky Balboa? Who ran in snowshoes?

So far, though, other than the increase in her stride, nothing seemed to be out of the ordinary. No other tracks anywhere near the path in the newly fallen snow from that morning, no signs of blood to indicate she'd been injured, and she had stayed on the packed snow of the trail where they obviously came out here daily.

The poles saved him from falling more than once, but he continued forward. The gaiter that covered his neck, mouth, and nose made him feel like he suffocated as his breathing became more rapid. His calves burned, and his fingers ached from the cold.

"Hazel!" Barry's voice shouted from somewhere behind

him, the sound muted by the evergreen trees surrounding him on all sides.

Mack sighed in relief, thanking his stars that the guys had arrived. They knew the land better than him, and if she was hurt, they'd be able to help him carry her back to the cabin. However, he kept moving forward. One foot in front of the other. No doubt, they'd catch up to him.

To his right, the sound of a snowmobile approaching nearly caused him to stumble. Obviously, at least one of the guys had decided to shovel in front of the shed to go gas-powered. However, the noise passed by without him ever seeing anyone.

Footsteps approached quickly behind him, and he stopped to look back. The face wasn't visible, but the guy's height and build made him think—beneath the gear—it was probably Barry. And the guy wore a set of the unusual snow-shoes similar to the prints he followed, which were obviously —now that he'd seen them—meant for running. On the pack he carried, though, was a different set of snowshoes with spikes.

"Up ahead, this trail is going to split into a figure-eight formation. I'll go left. You go right. When you get to the middle juncture, go right again. Vin is taking the snowmobile up to the farthest point of the trail. If we haven't found her by then, we'll regroup there." Barry bounced in place as he stopped behind him on the trail. He reached in his pocket and pulled out a small airhorn-like canister. "Mack, if you find her or if you get hurt, set this off. Do one blast. Wait two minutes for the second blast. Wait five more minutes for the last one. These things don't hold a lot."

"Got it. One blast. Two minutes. Another blast. Five minutes. Last blast," Mack noted, fumbling to put the container in his pocket.

Barry nodded and patted him on the shoulder. "Good man. Let's go."

Feeling pressured, Mack moved to the side of the path. "You go ahead. It took me twenty minutes to do what took you five."

Without further encouragement, Barry took off ahead of him and veered left. With adrenaline pumping, Mack power-walked and took the right trail. He studied the ground, reassured that he still saw her snowshoe prints. He should have looked to the left to see if Barry's tracks were the only ones there, but he hadn't thought of it.

The snow wasn't as deep under the trees, but the trail also didn't feel as firm. Less snow obviously filtered through the forest canopy. He imagined the sun also didn't penetrate, meaning nothing melted the top layer of snow so it would refreeze harder and create a crust.

The path started to turn left again, moving him toward that center point. However, he spotted a few of the trees with broken branches, and the snow had been trampled down to dirt in places. Lots of big animals had gone through this area.

How big were mountain lions exactly? Did bears roam in packs like wolves? Next time he travelled, he really needed to do more research on things in the area that could kill him.

The terrain became more difficult to navigate with the snow broken and trampled. It slowed his progress, but finally, he came out of the trees and saw where the path merged together before splitting off again. In front and to his left, Barry held out a hand to stop him without looking in his direction. Mack paused and scanned the area that had captured the other man's interest.

He froze.

Bison? Buffalo? Whatever they were, they were fucking huge, and they were probably two hundred feet away.

He'd seen movies, and sure, in the movies, the buffalo

were larger than the horses the people were riding. It never occurred to him *how much* bigger, though, until he came face to face with a herd of thirty to fifty of them. They'd circled up with the smaller ones in the middle, though smaller was such a relative term in this scenario. The smallest he could see was probably three hundred pounds.

Slightly to his right but with half of the herd between them, Hazel stood with her back against one of the few standing trees in that area. She was just off the path, and she cradled her right arm against her stomach. However, when she noticed him looking, she pulled her gaiter down so he could see her lips moving.

Slow, she mouthed, motioning him backward. *Slow.*

The herd shifted nervously as a wolf howled too close. He scanned around them, but he didn't see any wolves. However, he noticed droplets of blood in the snow. The pinkish red dots mostly seemed to be in the center of the herd, not near Hazel.

Barry had also started to motion him away. Carefully, he took one step backward then another and another. Without turning his back on the massive animals, he continued moving toward the trail he'd just come down. Only, he'd forgotten that the animals had churned up the path, and his snowshoe twisted in a rut.

Mack landed flat on his back as multiple howls cut the air, all on the other side of the herd. The buffalo grunted and shifted, their nerve starting to break. He tried to roll onto his side, but with the gear and snowshoes, he couldn't seem to move. He probably looked like an upside-down turtle.

Barry cursed, and Mack struggled again to get up. He turned his head to the side to see one of the large beasts charging toward Barry. Luckily, the guy was quick on his snowshoes and dodged to the side—farther from where Mack lay. He waved his arms and yelled, causing the buffalo to pause before charging again. The noise sounded weirdly like a roar, but it was hard to tell with a chorus of howls in the background.

The shuffling of the herd became louder, and the ground trembled. Lifting his head, he saw that the buffalo were running directly toward him.

CHAPTER 6

Hazel had been locked in stasis with the herd for closing on an hour. As she'd circled back toward the cabin, the large group of female bison had wandered across the trail. She'd stopped immediately. Unfortunately, the circling wolf pack had injured one of the yearling bison, and since this particular herd was descended from wild bison and not released, tamed ones, they still had the instincts to circle their weaker members to protect them.

The matriarch of these cows, whom Hazel had nicknamed Big Mama, had become really testy about the mix of strong wolf scent and light bear scent. She'd charged Hazel, and one of her horns had caught her arm. Though the break had healed, she'd need Barry to rebreak it and set it properly for it to heal correctly.

Across the way, Mack had fallen, and Barry dodged another testy cow. Nearby, the wolf pack was growing impatient as the smell of blood grew stronger. The injured animal's cries had stopped a while ago. Sadly, this stand was for nothing. Like most ungulates, the bison herd's nerve would only hold so long before fear caused them to break

BEAR HUG | 69

and run. Then the wolves could have their feast, and the people could get back into the warmth of the cabin, because damn, Hazel wanted her chair by the fire.

The howls mixed with Barry's roar, and Hazel felt the change in the air. Her developing bear instincts warned her, and she searched for Big Mama in the shuffling masses. The cows were going to stampede, fleeing from the biggest danger stalking them—the wolves. Their path would flow toward the area of least threat—Mack.

Hazel kicked the snow off her snowshoes and sprinted toward where Mack lay. Perhaps, her adding herself to the path would deter the herd. Maybe the light scent of a predator from TTV in her veins would make them move. Probably, she was about to be trampled along with her sweet journalist who had come looking for her.

Their nerve held until the howls of the pack echoed in the clearing. Luckily, her months of training in the snow and the paranormal blood in her veins boosted her speed. She half-slid to a stop at Mack's feet, turning toward the oncoming herd and waving her uninjured arm as they charged. Like Barry, she screamed and bounced in place, hoping the noise and movement would startle them.

Too late, Big Mama changed trajectory. The herd was too big, though. They would miss Barry completely, but at least a third of them wouldn't be able to avoid Hazel and Mack. That many horns and hooves and, heck, sheer weight would be fatal.

"Shift, goddamn it!" Barry screamed at her, still waving his arms as he ran toward her. "Shift!"

Not pausing to question him, Hazel reached for the brown bear lingering under her skin, in her blood, mixed with her soul. The adrenaline and fear pumping through her body must have motivated her Ursus side, because her shift came faster than ever before. The constricting clothing shredded as the massive form burst forth, the pressure of changing inside the snowsuit causing her to scream at the discomfort. Her human brain realized that was the reason the members of her arktoi always stripped before shifting.

The first horn caught her side as the last of her human shape disappeared. Forcing herself up onto two legs, she stretched as tall as she could and roared. The bison tried to split further, to avoid the massive predator who'd just appeared in their path, but they moved too fast and were too large to shift on a dime.

As she fell, she twisted so that she caught herself above Mack. Her paw caught his shoulder as she landed, and he screamed in pain. Bracing herself as hooves and horns pummeled her, her only concern was keeping her body above his and her weight off him. The pain hurt worse than any fight injury she'd ever suffered but not nearly as bad as the accident that had led her to become a bear in the first place.

In those long seconds, Hazel tried to concentrate on Mack's face. However, the fear and horror she saw made her turn away. Then the last of the bison passed, but she couldn't move. If she tried to move, she would fall on top of the man she'd tried to protect.

"It's okay, Hazelbear. I'm going to pull him out," Barry assured her, touching her shoulder gently. "You are doing great, Hazel. Like an old pro. The boss man is going to be really proud of your control... Mack, put your uninjured arm above your head."

Hazel kept her head turned away, but she sensed the movement beneath her as Mack moved his arm. Then he slid slowly away from her as Barry grabbed him and tugged.

"All clear. He's clear."

Without conscious thought, Hazel collapsed. A grunt of pain escaped, and she tried to reach for the human skin

BEAR HUG | 71

inside of her. However, it was gone. She closed her eyes and cried out in panic.

"Hey, hey," Barry murmured soothingly, his hand on her head. Somehow, the touch of her arktoi member eased a little of the pain and brought her comfort. He didn't let go. "It is okay. You're just tired and hurt. You need a minute to heal before you can shift again. You've never been hurt in this form before, and you've never tried two quick-shifts in a row. Patience, kiddo."

Behind her, an airhorn sounded. Her body heaved as she tried to stand, but other than the lightning rod of pain running through her, nothing moved. Then the noise sounded again, echoing off the snowbanks. Her heart rammed against her chest, and her paw shook as she tried to push her body upwards.

Barry cursed above her head. "It's okay, Hazelbear. It's okay. Shh. The wolves were getting bold and trying to come into the clearing for their kill, but Mack scared them back. Plus, that noise will bring Vin, and he'll be able to help."

In the distance, the motor of a snowmobile grew louder. She breathed deeply, but she could only smell the comforting scent of Barry and the overwhelming odor of blood and meat from the dead bison. Her stomach growled, and her brother-by-love laughed. "This really screwed with your vegetarianism. Don't worry. We'll get you a nice protein-filled fruit shake when we get back to the cabin. You'll forget all about how much you want to join the wolves for lunch, yeah?"

Hazel huffed, knowing he was right. The thought of fresh meat both turned her stomach and caused her mouth to water. The knowledge that the animal that died had only lived a year hurt her heart. Male or female, it could have done so much for the growing herds in the area.

"Fuck," Vin grunted, approaching.

"Herd of..." Barry began, but Vin waved him to silence

before placing his hand on Hazel's neck. Her entire body relaxed further, and she laid her head on the ground beside her Abilo's feet.

"Not important right now. Why don't you and the journalist head back to the cabin?"

Barry cleared his throat, prepared to argue, but Vin looked at him. Standing, Barry pulled off his backpack and rifled through it. He handed an emergency blanket—rolled tightly—to Vin, and then he changed out his special snowshoes for the more traditional ones on his back. Through it all, Vin stroked Hazel's ears.

"Let's go, Mack," Barry ordered. "It's going to be a long walk back, and we need to get you under a hot shower."

Mack, though, stood with his back to them. The airhorn canister was still clutched in his hand. "No. Someone has to watch for the wolves. We can't leave her here without someone to watch for the wolves or the mountain lions or the b-bears. The other bears."

Vin sighed, resigned. "Okay. Barry, go over there and help him watch for predators."

Then he rubbed his hand over Hazel's rounded ears, between her eyes, and down her snout. Hazel felt his energy surrounding her with his touch, and those fingers of warmth found the human shape hiding under the fur and commanded her to change back.

Her bones snapped. The blood in her veins boiled. Her hair follicles burned. The world turned dark. Then nothing hurt at all.

TWO DAYS LATER, HER DOOR SHOOK AS MACK KNOCKED ON it hard enough she questioned the integrity of the hinges. Sitting in the corner of her bed hugging her pillow, Hazel silently stared at the wall. She needed him

BEAR HUG | 73

to go away. She also wanted him to come in. But most of all, she just wished Mack didn't know she was a monster.

"Hazel, it's obvious you are conscious. If you aren't, your team has been bringing meals in, eating the food themselves, and taking empty dishes to the kitchen. I've watched these guys eat, and you all do not dine from the same menus," Mack called through the door.

The chuckle bubbled out before she could stop it, and she covered her mouth.

"I like that sound," he murmured. "Will you come out now? Please talk to me."

She sighed, wanting to see his face and knowing he would be leaving on a flight to Las Vegas early in the morning. Paolo, their Bruin, had arrived yesterday to check on her. He'd also brought a witch, who had sworn Mack to secrecy on the existence of the paranormal in a ceremony Hazel hadn't witnessed. However, Barry and David both assured her that Mack had agreed to it without hesitation. Then the witch had healed the shoulder Hazel'd dislocated trying to save him.

Slipping her feet into her house shoes and pulling on her robe over her pajamas, she smoothed down her hair before opening the door a crack. He'd leaned his head against the center of the wooden door, and only his grip on the frame kept him from falling forward. The smile on his face faded as he looked at her.

"You've been crying," he murmured. "Barry said you'd healed, that your arm was even better. He went on a run with that king guy, but I can try to find them."

His concern warmed Hazel, and she touched his wrist on the arm she'd injured before pulling back. "I'm sorry I hurt you. I try hard not to be a bad person. And the guys aren't bad people. I hope you know that."

Mack's forehead crinkled, and he blinked as he tilted his head slightly. "Hazel, you saved my life."

Tears filled her eyes, and she wiped them away as frustration overflowed. "It isn't saving your life if looking for me was what endangered your life to begin with."

Leaning forward, his arms wrapped her in a hug. Startled, she stiffened. Then she hugged him back. The emotions of the last two days boiled over, and she buried her face in his shoulder. The sobs shook her body, but he only squeezed tighter.

"Hazel, you are the kindest person I've ever met, and I've met a lot of people. No one who's been around you more than a minute—outside an octagon, at least—will ever have anything negative to say about you." He rubbed her back in soothing circles. "Your other half literally survived being trampled by the biggest herd of buffa…"—he paused and corrected himself—"bison I have ever seen while managing not to crush me beneath you. And the guys tell me that you gave up your career not because you worry about yourself but because you worry about the people you'd face. That the fight would endanger them and also wouldn't be fair. I just… I don't know how to tell you how much I admire you and respect you."

Hazel leaned back and smiled. Relief eased the tightness in her chest. He didn't hate her for all that happened, for her actions leading to him being injured and then a literal spell cast on him. She would accept the blame, because it was her fault. But she still wanted him to be her friend.

"When you came to Colorado, did you ever imagine the weekend you'd have?" she murmured.

The lines around his eyes and mouth tightened a moment. Then light filled his face once again, and he grinned as he gave her a squeeze. "Pardon my saying, but I never imagined the lengths you'd run to get me in a bear hug."

She leaned forward and kissed his cheek. "Maybe once your journalistic integrity is no longer in question, I can show you a front naked chokehold."

Brushing his thumb over her lips, he leaned his forehead against hers and breathed her scent.

"A fight to the finish," he agreed.

CHAPTER 7

Mack yawned and rubbed his eyes, blinking rapidly to clear his vision. The wave of sleepiness hit suddenly, despite the extra black, double shot of espresso coffee he'd finished five minutes ago. The second yawn caused him to drive onto the rumble strip on the side of the road, and he nearly overcorrected getting back on it.

With a sigh, knowing he was only about an hour away from Vincent's cabin, he decided to take the exit for Eiffel Creek. Worst case scenario, he'd grab a two-hour nap in the car somewhere relatively safe and then drive the last seventy miles. Also, please God, let there be somewhere with more coffee. Maybe a caffeine IV.

When his GPS had said the drive would take twelve hours with traffic, it hadn't accounted for the three accidents between Las Vegas and Colorado Springs. One had taken almost two hours to clear. He should have arrived around supper time, running on the logic that—even if Hazel kicked him out—someone would feed him before making him leave.

As he drove into the town, he realized that "town" was an optimistic descriptor. The first building he passed had been closed for years, reminiscent of a gas station from times gone by where an attendant pumped the gas for people. Ahead and to his right, a well-lit parking lot lured him down the single lane road.

As far as he could tell, the only other lights were streetlamps and not many of those. No other businesses appeared to be open at 10 p.m., and he didn't see a single yellow arch, crowned king of burgers, or fast-food joint cutting the darkness of the night.

He sighed, accepting that his options were limited.

Pulling into the parking lot of the Howling Moon Bar and Grill, he sat in the car for a long moment trying to decide whether he wanted to go in or keep driving. The tiredness had disappeared the moment he took the exit, like magic, but every time he thought about turning around and driving on, a yawn threatened to dislocate his jaw.

Maybe this bar serves coffee? he thought, grabbing his coat, keys, and wallet from the passenger seat.

In the two months since he'd left the cabin and flown back to Vegas, the weather hadn't improved. Luckily, the transportation department here stayed ahead of the snow, unlike in Nevada where a single snowflake shut down the state. He'd seen a few bright orange signs closing exits and side roads, but nothing forcing him to reroute yet.

Muted sounds of laughter and music drifted through the door, which looked like it could hold off an avalanche if it became necessary. He glanced over his shoulder, relieved to see the dark outline of the nearest mountains much too far away to dump a deadly amount of snow on them. As a bonus, there wasn't a single bison in sight.

Warm air greeted him when he opened the door, but the music wasn't as loud as the noise outside implied. He walked between the people shooting billiards to his left and patrons drinking at the high-top tables to his right, heading straight toward the bartender behind the bar. Having been to many bars in Vegas, he felt comfortable ranking this one as the cleanest he'd ever set foot inside. No mysterious stains on the floor that might or might not be blood, no sticky goop on the side of the bar that could be something worse, and no rank puddles of less mysterious green pee in the corners.

"What can I get you?" the bartender asked, popping the tops off four beers and putting them in a bucket with ice. He passed them across the shiny counter to the man glaring at Mack as though he'd stepped on the dude's kitten when he entered.

"Do you have coffee?" Mack asked, not retreating from the angry stranger out of pure stubbornness. Finally, the guy moved away to one of the high tops.

"No, but if you are looking for caffeine, we have fountain sodas."

"A soda is good," Mack agreed. *Better than water or beer, at least.*

"Pepsi okay?"

Mack nodded, moving to sit on the stool. He laid his jacket across his lap and the keys on the counter.

The man placed a short glass with ice in front of him and used the soda gun to fill it. "You're not one of my regulars. Passing through or here on business?"

Mack sipped his drink and shook his head. "On my way shortly. A bad case of exhaustion hit me right before your exit. I'd hoped to grab a cup of coffee and get back on the road."

"Oh?" The man suddenly looked interested. "Sorry about the coffee. The whole town basically rolls up by nine o'clock, and the only hot coffee would be at the diner when it opens at six A.M." The bartender stuck out his hand, which he accepted after wiping the condensation from the glass on his jeans. "I'm Miguel."

BEAR HUG | 79

"Mack."

They shook twice. Then Miguel moved down the counter to take an order. Mack glanced over his right shoulder, and a number of people glared at him. Turning back to his glass, he tucked his head and finished the drink. However, before he could wave him away, Miguel refilled the rocks glass. "Ignore them. You see, we have way more men than women in this little town. When a lady joins our numbers? Jubilation. Another guy, though? Doesn't matter how brief you intend to stay. You're competition."

Mack nodded, pulling a ten-dollar bill from his wallet and sliding it across the counter. "I'll finish this glass, use your restroom, and be on my way. Hopefully the stop and caffeine boost can get me a couple more hours."

Miguel grinned at him, as though he knew something Mack didn't. However, the bartender took the cash to the register and hit a couple buttons. As the bartender counted the change, it seemed a good time to use the bathroom and get on the road again. Mack grabbed his jacket and keys, sliding the first over his shoulder and the second in his pocket. Then he slammed back the last of the soda and headed toward the sign in the back left corner.

Head down, he could feel eyes on him and decided to watch his feet. He quickly turned the corner into the bathroom hallway, wanting to be out of the line of sight. His progress stopped abruptly as he bumped into someone, his hands reaching out to steady them even as his jacket hit the—luckily, super-clean—floor.

"I am so sorry," she started, her hands holding his arm almost too tight as she caught her balance. "I should have been watching…"

He froze, looking up. His heartrate kicked up as though a day's worth of caffeine hit his system all at once. For a moment, he felt light-headed. "Holy shit. Hazel?"

Her eyes lit up as she let go of his arm and wrapped him up in a hug. "Mack! What are you doing here?" She rocked him back and forth, holding him as though she didn't want to let him go.

The surprise wore off, and he hugged her back. "I was driving up to the cabin to test my welcome."

She leaned back, her forehead wrinkled as she studied him. "And you just decided to pit stop at an exit with no posted signs for food or hotels or gas? You like to live dangerously. Not that I'm ungrateful. It's wonderful to see you!"

He laughed, raising his hand to touch her cheek and smooth the lines. "The most dangerous thing I've done in my life is fall in love with a bear, uh,"—he paused and realized people stood at the tables not far away—"a beautiful woman. A very beautiful woman. I'm here because I needed a jolt of adrenaline to finish the trip to see her." As she stepped back, tugging on her braid nervously, her eyes darted down to his coat, and she bent to pick it up.

"You got a good one. Rated for the cold here." Shaking it out, she handed it to him and bit her lip. "Does that maybe mean you plan to stay a while?"

He tucked the coat under his arm. "Maybe we should have this discussion somewhere else?" Tilting his head toward the bathroom door, he raised his eyebrows.

Hazel laughed, pointing toward the restroom, and he savored the sound. "I think you were on your way in. I'll put my pool opponent out of his misery, and you can come find me."

He leaned forward and kissed her lips. Then he headed at a fast pace toward the men's room as she chuckled behind him. When he finished washing his hands, he checked himself in the mirror. Even his reflection looked better in this bar than in regular bar mirrors. He ran his slightly damp

BEAR HUG | 81

fingers through his hair to try to bring it to order before going back into the main room.

As he stepped out, Hazel finished folding her pool stick into a case as a group of guys tried to convince her to stay longer. Their good-natured cajoling carried to him as he put on his jacket. She smiled at their begging and shrugged into her puffy coat, zipping it as the three all talked at once. With a chuckle, she patted them on the shoulders as she stepped away. Seeing him, she waved and motioned him toward the door. He hurried in her direction, arriving only seconds after her.

"You mind driving? It's only a minute up the road," she assured him as he held the bar door open. "I walked. I didn't want to risk drinking alcohol and driving, even for such a short distance."

He snorted, moving around the car to open the passenger door for her. "I planned to drive an hour and a half more to get to you. A minute is less than nothing."

She sat and pulled her legs inside. Mack waited an extra second, making sure she was clear of the door before he shut it. He glanced through the windshield as he speed-walked to the driver's side. The light shined in the window, and he saw her watching him back. The silence in the car was loud as he climbed in and buckled his seatbelt. She clutched the pool stick case like it was a life raft and she was stranded in the middle of the ocean.

He put the keys in the ignition, his hand shaking slightly, and started the car. The air from the vents had already cooled. Quickly, he turned the blower speed down. Putting the car in reverse, he looked over his shoulder to back up. She waited until he shifted to drive before cutting through the awkwardness.

"Mack, how did you end up in Eiffel Creek? And why didn't you call to tell me you were coming?"

A quick peek at her reassured him that she seemed confused, not angry. "I tried calling. Phone went straight to voicemail, so I decided to head up on hope. A sudden case of the yawns brought me to this exit for a cup of coffee and a nap, though the adrenaline from running into you woke me up."

She chuckled. "Oh? Pure luck then?"

"Apparently," he agreed, pulling to the road. "How'd you get here?"

She motioned for him to turn right. "Speed limit is thirty-five through town, but I saw the sheriff having a beer at Rafferty's place," she admitted.

To be safe, he checked his speedometer and kept it right between thirty and forty. Being locked in with Hazel for longer wasn't exactly a hardship.

"The location of Vin's cabin is public knowledge for anyone who does the right research, which means it isn't really a safe hideout for me. The arktoi have opted to move here, though Vin kept his cabin for his own sanity."

The slow drive allowed him to notice almost all the streetlights glowed red, and he did a double take.

"Bats. I've learned so much about bats in my month here. Colorado has eighteen species of bats, they eat something like six hundred bugs an hour, and their favorite food is my least favorite insects—mosquitos. Since Eiffel Creek is quite eco-conscious, they converted all of the streetlights to red bulbs some years ago, because bats are just as active in red lights as they are at night but less active—and eat fewer bugs —when there are regular lights." She pointed. "That's my driveway."

He signaled and slowed down. "I've never even seen a bat in real life."

When he stopped behind the gray SUV in her driveway, he glanced at the house as he put his car in park and turned it off. His headlights caught the siding of the house. "Is your house... mint?"

"Oh, Mack, you are in for a treat in the daylight. Houses here are either colorful or log cabin. No in-between. My house is mint, and David and Barry's bachelor pad three houses down is wicked-witch green. Vin's would best be described as orchid, and I think he chose it because he is secretly a delicate flower," she joked.

"Orchid? Vincent?" he asked, trying to mesh the gruff older man and any cultivated flower.

Her laugh brought a smile to his face, and she winked at him as the headlights automatically shut off. "He's just a teddy bear under that grizzly exterior." Then she sighed and gripped the handle. "Okay. Ready?"

He nodded. "Ready."

They both opened the door at the same time. Waiting until she came around the car, he followed her up the sidewalk. Only she stopped abruptly. He put his hands on her arms to keep from bumping into her—a third time—but she turned in his grip, her face concerned. "Don't you have a suitcase? Do you need me to borrow some of the guys' clothing?"

Mack cleared his throat and scuffed his shoe against the concrete. "I—uh—didn't want to presume you were inviting me to crash here."

Gently, she pushed him back toward the car. "Please get your suitcase. First of all, I'm the only one with an extra bedroom if you want privacy. Second, Vin is off with Paolo— the man who brought the witch to the cabin. Third, David flew to California for a meeting, and Barry is probably already in bed. Fourth, this town doesn't have a hotel or an inn or a motel. It actually doesn't even have a gutter for someone to get drunk and sleep it off in. Very shortsighted of them considering how popular the Howling Moon is."

He shook his head but popped his trunk using his key fob. Grabbing his suitcase, he slammed the lid closed and hurried to where she waited on the porch. "Howling Moon sounds like something a werewolf would name a business."

Her shoulder lifted in a shrug, and she raised her eyebrows at him pointedly. "Werewolf is a derogatory term. We are Ursus. They are Lykos."

His foot missed the step, and he stumbled. "Sorry. I was joking."

She opened the door, motioning him past. "Well, you kind of sleepwalked into their town—which has a long history we'll cover another day, sometime after we discuss whether you plan to stay and, if so, the specifics of pack hierarchy."

Mack swallowed, pausing inside the doorway to remove his shoes and take off his jacket. He set down his suitcase near the wall, out of the way. "Entire town of were—Lykos?"

She closed the door and patted his shoulder before bending over to unzip her heeled boots. "Almost entirely. Except four bears, a couple humans, an assortment of not-human but non-shifters, and one incorporeal witch."

He opened his mouth and closed it, his brain trying to process the sentence she'd strung together and then giving up. "That sounds like a conversation for after I sleep."

She picked up her boots and gestured to the room they were standing in. "This is the living room, and through there is the dining room. The laundry room is by the back door. There's a guest bathroom, a guest bedroom, and the master bedroom through the kitchen."

The walls were white, and she hadn't hung pictures yet. However, the exposed wooden beams in the ceiling and a couple inset shelves were natural pops of color. Her light gray couch and two matching chairs looked new but comfortable, and the coffee table had a copy of the article he had written and a stack of coasters lying on it. His bold head-

BEAR HUG | 85

line was a dead giveaway—"Crash and Overcome: Undefeated to the End."

"Did you read it?" he murmured, gesturing vaguely.

She glanced toward the table too. "I read it."

He exhaled, stepping closer to her and touching her arm to urge her to look at him. "Did you hate it?"

Her eyes shone as the light glinted off the tears filling them. "Mack, you made me sound like someone else. Like a superhero or a saint."

His hand skimmed down her arm until he entwined his fingers with hers. "I told the truth—well, within the limits of what the witch's spell allowed me. Name one thing I said that was a lie," he dared.

She hesitated. "Well, you didn't *lie*, but you embellished the truth. I'm not the 'nicest person in the world' or 'most humble undefeated fighter in MMA.' Those are sweet opinions, not facts."

Crowding her, he prompted, "But you didn't hate it."

Her lower lip trembled, and she leaned toward him, lifting her chin slightly. "How could I when what you wrote showed me that you'd forgiven me for endangering you? For being... what I am."

"Kind?" he asked, studying her mouth. "Compassionate?" He squeezed her hand in his before bringing it to his mouth and kissing her knuckles. "Strong." His other hand moving to her hip emphasized his statement. "Intelligent." She gripped his shoulder, her lips parting in invitation. "Sexy," he whispered as she closed her eyes.

Her rapid breathing mingled with his as he kissed her softly. The fingers on his shoulder tightened, and she jerked him closer. "Hazel Rei Metcalf," he choked out, "what you are is perfect. Every inch of every form—fighter, glue holding your family together, friend, pool shark... and bear. You are so damn perfect that I fell in love with you the first time I bumped into you. I didn't know it until I had to leave you behind at a cabin in the middle of the arctic tundra and realized that I cared more for you than I hated the snow." He grinned, leaning forward to kiss her gently—nothing more than his lips brushing hers. "And I hate the snow a whole fucking lot, Hazelbear."

She sighed softly, one of the tears that threatened earlier spilling down her cheek. "I'm sorry."

"That I love you?" he asked, freezing in place.

"No!" She tugged her fingers from his and cupped his cheeks. "I'm sorry that I'm going to ask you to stay here where we average over a hundred inches of snow a year, because I missed you so much these last two months that I never want you to leave. I love you too, Mack."

With a shout, he wrapped his arms around her waist and lifted her up. "Yes. Yes, I'll stay. Because the only thing I hate more than the snow is being without you."

The boots in her hand thumped to the floor. Her hands gripped his shoulders, and she enjoyed feeling the hardness of his muscles through his soft t-shirt. Leaning forward, her lips brushed his cheek then chin before finding his mouth. The moment their lips touched, his hold slipped.

Her body slid down his, but their kiss only deepened as he pulled her closer. When her feet touched the ground, she stepped slowly backward and tugged him along, through the dining room and kitchen toward the master bedroom. He pulled away to jerk his shirt over his head by the hem, and she began unbuttoning her blouse. Impatient, his fingers tangled with hers as he tried to help. Distracted, her back hit the wall, and she giggled in surprise.

He laughed, resting his forehead against hers. Exhaling shakily, he leaned his forehead against hers. "Time-out until we get to the bedroom?"

Her hand brushed over his side, exploring the exposed

BEAR HUG | 87

skin. With a light push, she guided him backward down the hallway. "I promised to teach you a front naked chokehold, and there's no time-outs until you tap," she challenged.

His Adam's apple bobbed as he swallowed hard, his gaze not leaving hers. The tightness in his chest and the droplets of sweat on his upper lip made him hyperfocused on the light reflecting from her eyes. However, when the backs of his legs hit the edge of her bed, he held his ground. "I won't tap. You're gonna have to make this a knockout."

The mischief in her eyes caused him to groan as she pushed him onto the bed. She finished the last couple buttons as he watched and dropped the blouse to the floor. Raising one eyebrow in challenge, her fingers unsnapped then unzipped her jeans. Mack raised himself up on his elbows as she stepped on the bottom of one pants leg then the other, walking out of them. "Let's see if I can make you pray for the bell to ring."

He unsnapped his own pants, trying to remove them without looking away from Hazel. "Never going to happen," he argued.

Her fingers reached behind her, and her bra loosened. For just a moment, her expression lightened in relief. Then the sultry expression returned as she wrapped an arm across her breasts to hold the cups up. One strap slid down her arm. Then the other fell. He groaned, scooting toward the edge of the bed to get up. She winked at him, and he hesitated as his heart stuttered. The bra hit the floor, and she shimmied the panties down her thighs.

"Never?" Hazel murmured, kneeling beside him on the bed.

"Mmm?" he asked, reaching for her as she straddled his thighs.

Her fingers wrapped around his cock, and his hold tightened on her waist. Leaning forward onto her free hand, she stroked him slowly, and he groaned.

Squeezing gently, she continued stroking him. Her thumb smoothed the precum over his tip, and his hips thrust up. "Hazel…"

She chuckled softly. "That sounded a little like a prayer, Mack."

For a second, his brain cleared. He pulled his legs up, and Hazel shifted slightly. In triumph, he bumped her forward in an MMA move he'd seen many times and then rolled her beneath him. Their bodies moved in sync, and then he held himself above her. "But not for the bell, gorgeous."

His mouth caressed her nipple, already pebbled despite the heat in the room. Her skin tasted sweet, like strawberries and cream, as he licked and nipped. His hand cupped her neglected breast, fingers lightly pinching as she cried out beneath him.

"Yes! Harder," she urged, her hand around his cock slowing at the distraction.

Mack moved his licks and nips to the other breast, and his hand slowly caressed down her ribs and over her stomach to rest above her abdomen. "Hazel?" he growled against the skin of her throat, a prayer.

"Please. Yes. Touch me!" she ordered.

Even now, she grappled for control. He couldn't help but chuckle as his hand swept lower. His fingers found her center, wet for him, and he brushed his thumb across her clitoris. For a moment, her grip on his cock tightened enough to take his breath, but she eased up as his middle finger slid inside her.

His mouth moved to explore her nipple again, sucking in time to his thrusts. Above him, her breath caught. "Mack…"

"God, yes," he agreed, speeding the movement of his fingers inside her. She half-rose from the bed, her free arm wrapping around his shoulder and fingers tangling in the short hair of his head. She pulled his mouth to hers.

"Inside me," she whispered against his mouth, urging him up. "I'm on the pill. We can't carry STIs. I'm safe," she promised.

Right then, he didn't care. He knew he should, but he couldn't tell her no now.

As he moved his fingers out and slid his cock inside her, he leaned forward to kiss her. Her hands explored his body, and his fingers stroked her clit. Against his mouth, her breath caught. Speeding the movement of his strokes, he pulled back to see her better. The pleasure on her face melted his heart.

"Come for me, Hazel."

Her fingers dug into his hips, and she wrapped her legs around his waist. He used both arms to keep from crushing her, matching her pace. The little wrinkles on her forehead deepened as her gasps grew shallower. Her body tightened around his cock, and he closed his eyes as the pleasure mixed with the pain of delayed gratification.

"Come now, Mack," she ordered, her grip shifting from his hip to his ass.

Her words mixed with her touch pushed him over the edge, and he gasped her name as he came. Her leg ran down the back of his as she unwrapped from around him with a satisfied smile. Carefully, he lowered himself down beside her. He paused halfway down to kiss her, and she sighed softly.

"I love you, Hazel," he murmured, wrapping his arm around her and holding her close.

"I love you too, Mack," she whispered, kissing his chin before snuggling down against him.

As he fell asleep, he decided she was still undefeated, but

90 | THIA MACKIN

he put up hell of a fight. Even losing made him a winner here, wrapped in her love.

"HAZELBEAR! YOU AREN'T GOING TO FUCKING BELIEVE THIS!" someone shouted from the living room. "Also, whose car is outside?"

The voice sounded louder by the word, and Mack groaned softly at the disturbance, enjoying the warm body curled against him. Her leg thrown over his and her arm draped across his chest, she'd become a living blanket who snored very softly.

"Hazel, who's here? And how are you still aslee—Oh, God bless, what the fuck?" Barry covered his eyes with one hand to hide the sight in the bedroom, turned, and beat his head softly against the wall before bringing the phone back to his ear. "I'm going to have to stab out my eyes now. David, you owe me—something. I can't even think of any payment enough to cover this."

Hazel's body shook, and he looked at her face in alarm. However, she chortled with glee.

Thankfully.

"Barry, I was fully covered. Calm down," she managed.

"She thinks this is funny! She was in bed with someone, and she thinks this is funny!" Barry exclaimed to David, affronted.

Mack wiped his eyes, wrapping his other arm around Hazel and holding her close beneath the covers. "Weren't you going to tell her something unbelievable?"

Barry glanced their way then turned his back toward them and faced the kitchen. "David tried to call you, but the service here wouldn't let him through. He had to dial Rafferty at the bar and have him forward the call. David's on his way to the airport, and he's flying back. You'll never believe what he found out."

"I agree. I'll never believe it." Hazel snuggled closer to Mack and tugged the cover up to her neck. "What is it?"

Suddenly completely serious, Barry turned toward her, phone at his side. "Bantamweight Champion Michaela Quinn is a Bouda, a hyena therianthrope. She was bitten fifteen years ago."

The body against his froze. Then she exploded from the bed, taking the comforter with her. In a panic, he snagged the bedsheet and pulled it over himself.

"That dishonorable, disgraceful, vile bitch!" Hazel exclaimed, throwing open her dresser drawers and grabbing items of clothing. She stormed into the bathroom and half-closed the door. Mack didn't realize Hazel even knew the words she was using, but it only impressed him. "That demon is endangering innocent people! She's old enough that she could turn them, right?"

"She is." Barry leaned against the doorframe, studying Mack where he sat on the edge of the bed trying to locate his pants. Mack finally spotted them between the chest of drawers and the wall. With a shrug, he left the sheet on the bed and moved to pull on his jeans.

"How dare that hyena-faced cheat use her paranormal strength to compete against humans!" Hazel accused, stomping out of the bathroom in leggings and a loose t-shirt. "Doesn't the community see that she risks exposing them? And what if she accidentally kills a human? Or worse, infects them without their consent. Someone has to stop her!"

Barry held up the phone in his hand, the speaker button lit up on the screen, and wiggled it. He grinned before saying, "Hey, Bear Hug, your manager wants to know how you feel about coming out of retirement for one last fight? Turns out, Quinn swore to her Qora—her nobility—that she would stop fighting when she no longer had her title to defend. Their monarch—their Mfalme—wants her out of the ring before it's too late."

Hazel stopped pacing, her head turning slowly toward Barry—more like a snake scenting prey than any bear Mack had ever seen. "Then her Mfalme should get what she wants. Let's take her title."

"You sure?" Barry and David asked together.

David continued. "Hazelbear, you haven't fought in an octagon in a very long time."

Mack raised his hand, certain he'd followed the key elements of the conversation. "What she has done in the meantime is better. She's practiced against two Ursus who matched her strength, who didn't have to pull their punches. She has trained to take down a Bouda—isn't that someone who changes to a hyena in folklore?—without knowing that was where fate steered her."

Barry nodded.

David grunted. "Yeah, well, we're gonna train some more. I'm going to call Vin, see if Paolo will approve it, and then I'll call World Fighting Inc. and get it headlined. We'll publicize this as—win or lose—Bear Hug's final fight."

"'Phoenix or Finished: Trial by TKO,'" Mack murmured. "The headlines practically write themselves."

Hazel crossed the room to him, wrapping her arms around his waist and leaning her head against his shoulder. Her heart still pounded with the overflow of that earlier anger; without thought, he rubbed soothing circles at the small of her back.

"Mack, I'm not sure if covering the fight would make you uncomfortable, but I still want my good luck charm there. Will you come?"

Her eyes pleaded with him, and he kissed her. "You couldn't stop me. Remember? I'm part of the team."

EPILOGUE

Overhead, music blared and the crowd cheered to welcome her opponent onto the floor. The entrance theatrics had been rehearsed twice this past week after tickets to the event sold out. In fact, World Fighting Inc. had sent dozens of baskets and bouquets to their hotel suite as sales matched their previously highest-grossing men's heavyweight fight. Rumors swirled that the pay-per-view watches might push this once-in-a-lifetime fight over the edge into record-breaking territory.

"Duck and weave," Vincent ordered after they checked to make sure her mouth guard was in place. He rubbed petroleum jelly over her cheekbones and brows, covering the most likely points of impact on her face. The Vaseline made the skin more elastic and less likely to tear if struck.

Barry grabbed her shoulders, shaking her once in excitement. "Come on, Hazelbear. Take her down fast and hard, just like we practiced."

David eyed her then nodded, nodding toward the octagon. "Remember. Live up to your name. Kick her ass and give her the message you were charged with."

94 | THIA MACKIN

Hazel bounced in place twice and headed up the stairs. She paced around the ring, waving to the people who had traveled long distances and paid hard-earned money to witness her last fight. Smiling, she pretended the ones there to see her undefeated streak end didn't exist. Then the floor shook beneath her bare feet as someone ran up the stairs.

The smell of hundreds of bodies—many of whom had walked a decent distance under the Nevada sun— in small places like the hotel lobby and restaurants had made her nose blind for days. Tonight, though, her senses adjusted better. She smelled the sweat and blood stained into the ring, the overwhelming cologne of the referee who stood a short distance away, and the barest hint of dry grasses and feline fur wafting from the woman across from her. If she didn't know better, she'd think the woman had let a cat sleep on her fight apparel—not that she was a hyena therianthrope.

In the background, the music faded as the announcer's voice keyed up. "Greystone Arena welcomes all of you in this sold-out crowd as World Fighting Inc. presents three five-minute rounds for your entertainment. In the blue corner, standing five-feet-eight-inches and weighing 133 pounds with an undefeated 9-0 record, she hails from Colorado Springs, Colorado—Hazel 'Bear Hug' Metcalf!"

The announcer paused as the crowd roared, only continuing as the sound began to dim. "Across the cage, her adversary fights out of the green corner at five-feet-six-inches and 135 pounds. By way of Shreveport, Louisiana and fighting out of our very own Viva Las Vegas, the reigning and defending World Fighting Inc. bantamweight champion has fifteen wins and four losses. Introducing Michaela 'The Stunner' Quinn."

Roars echoed off the ceiling, and people stomped their feet and cheered for the obvious favorite. Across the mat, her opponent soaked up the adoration, and Hazel had to let the woman, not because Michaela'd earned it—because a therianthrope fighting humans had a seriously unfair advantage. Only because Hazel intended to take this from her forever... in a single round.

"When the bell rings, the referee in charge of the action is Luke Rance. Now let the fight begin!"

Rolling her shoulders, Hazel looked toward Luke. He'd handled a couple of her early matches, a true professional. Stepping away from the fence, he held his hand out toward her. "Ready?"

"Ready!"

He stretched his arm toward Michaela. "Ready?"

"Ready!" she called, her eyes meeting Hazel's as they both raised their fists.

Luke nodded. "Fight!"

Immediately, the bell rang and noise fell away. Her vision focused on the woman in front of her, blocking out the referee, her team, and the thousands of people chanting in the background. She and Michaela both came to the middle and touched fingertips before retreating. Then the dance began.

For her entire career, Hazel'd come through as a knockout professional. She won by her solid punches and, twice, kicks. However, in the past two months since WFI's doctor had cleared her for the match and they'd put her name on the ticket, she and the team had practiced submission techniques until the moves became so ingrained that she'd accidentally thrown Mack out of bed one night for tossing his arm over her neck while they slept.

Dancing forward, she threw a punch toward Michaela's protected head. Raising her leg, Hazel blocked the kick. As she planted her foot again, Hazel jabbed into her opponent's side. Backing away, she tried to lure Michaela back toward the center of octagon. The Bouda came at her with a vengeance, throwing three quick punches. Hands up, Hazel protected her face but left her middle exposed.

Michaela charged her, wrapping her arms around Hazel's waist. Their feet tangled as the shorter woman attempted to take them to the mat. But it wasn't time for that yet. Instead, Hazel leaned forward over her, accepting the punches to the side as she brought her knee up into Michaela's face. The second time she connected, either blood or spit spattered her leg.

If I were human. If I hadn't been infected already... The quiet turned staticky, and Hazel reminded herself to let the anger go.

She ducked into Michaela's personal space, her jab missing the Bouda's head as she ducked down. Hazel felt the grip on her leg and prepared herself for the leg takedown; she'd stepped into it, literally, like an amateur.

However, Hazel wasn't the only one letting emotions cause stupid mistakes. Michaela followed her onto the ground, moving into a mount position. Pinning her on her back, the Bouda threw punches at Hazel's face. This move, though, they'd practiced. If she pulled her hands up, the situation would go south faster. Instead, she brought her legs closer to her body to create a base and lifted her hips to bump the Bouda forward. Moving her hands to Michaela's sides, Hazel turned laterally and created an arch from her opponent's legs that allowed her to pull her leg up and through. Bringing her knees in, she pulled Michaela into the guard position, Hazel's arms and legs crossed behind her.

The hyena therianthrope immediately punched the side of Hazel's head using the arm outside of the guard. For the first time in the fight, Michaela used her paranormal strength. The shot loosened Hazel's arms enough for the champion to partially escape the hold. She pushed her forearm into Hazel's chest and used her other fist to punch.

BEAR HUG | 97

Exhaling through the ringing in her ears, she swept Michaela's wrist off trajectory mid-motion, bringing her elbow behind the other woman's bicep. A hard pull forward brought the Bouda off-balance enough that Hazel held her down while bringing her own knees up—one over Michaela's shoulder and one under in a high guard. Hazel squeezed her legs together to control the other shifter's motion. Reaching her right hand under Michaela's left arm, Hazel gripped her own right shin with her left hand to trap her opponent in the hold.

The champion's hand struggled against her, unable to strike, and Hazel knew loosening her grip on the woman's arms would earn a punch to the face. Instead, she lifted her left leg up and behind the Bouda, resting across the woman's neck and over her back. She locked her right ankle over the left shin, trapping Michaela's right arm between their bodies at an awkward angle as Hazel squeezed her hips together. Leaning her torso up, Hazel gripped the woman's right hand with pressure on her thumb and tucked it against her shoulder. Then she leaned back, straining to keep the hold tight.

Michaela's entire body struggled, shaking as she fought the pain shooting down her arm but not wanting to give up. The seconds passed like hours as Hazel realized she might have to break the joint to make the Bouda tap out. Tensing in preparation, Hazel forced all the air out of her body.

Three soft taps against her right shoulder almost caused her to release Michaela in relief that the woman wouldn't force her to move from hurt to harm. However, Hazel waited until the referee came up and signaled her.

The bell rang.

Suddenly, the booming of the announcer shouting into the microphone and the shouting of thousands of people hit her. She nearly staggered, stumbling to the fence in her corner where her team waited. Vin grinned and handed her

98 | THIA MACKIN

the plastic container to put her mouthguard in, and she secured it before handing it back. David and Barry yelled at her, gesturing excitedly.

Then Hazel turned and met Michaela's eyes. After a few steps toward her, Michaela met her in the middle for a quick hug. Hazel leaned in, holding the Bouda in place as she lifted her gloved hand to cover the movement of her lips from the cameras. "Your Mfalme—your queen—says keep your promise. Or else."

She dropped her hand, relieved that the Bouda would no longer endanger humans or the paranormal community, and patted Michaela twice on the back. "Good fight!" she shouted over the noise.

Luke motioned them both over. He gripped her wrist in one hand and Michaela's in the other, the three standing almost shoulder to shoulder. The announcer's voice over the loudspeaker quieted the din of the audience. "Ladies and gentlemen, referee Luke Rance called a halt to this battle royale at two minutes and forty-two seconds of round one for your winner by submission via arm bar, the still undefeated, new Bantamweight Champion Hazel 'Bear Hug' Metcalf," the announcer shouted, bringing the crowd to their feet.

Luke raised Hazel's wrist in the air, and he released Michaela's to let her leave the ring. The owner of World Fighting Inc. stepped into the ring beside a beautiful woman in a sequined dress that sparkled almost as much as the bantamweight belt over her shoulder. He raised the microphone to his lips, introducing himself and lauding his company's achievements in cultivating such talented mixed martial artists. Finally, he asked, "Is Hazel 'Bear Hug' Metcalf really going to retire after the best fight of her career?" He leaned the microphone toward her.

"Turns out, ten-and-oh is my lucky number. I think it's a

good record for your other fighters to beat." Smiling for the cameras, she accepted the belt and held it over her head for everyone to see. Then Barry picked her up from behind and spun her as David lifted her arm in the air again.

Finally, her feet planted firmly on the mat, she turned toward the exit. They still needed to do the press circuit, the after-party, and the pay-per-view interview before she could crawl into bed tonight. Luckily, this venue had a nice dressing room with a shower where she could freshen up.

"You did good," Vin admitted. "Despite how impressive your knockouts are, you do have one mean bear hug."

She groaned, carefully walking down the stairs to prevent the people taking photos from catching her falling. Dozens of flashes went off a second, and the noise was still deafening. Hazel looked up, smiled, and waved slowly toward the crowd before stepping off the last step.

"Ms. Metcalf," a familiar voice said. "In light of your recent win, I hoped to cop another exclusive."

His voice kicked her heartbeat up a notch, and she turned toward Mack so fast she nearly stumbled. His grin matched hers as he admired the belt, walking close enough to touch the leather part. "You worked hard for this. Congratulations, Hazelbear."

She moved closer to him, until she needed to place her hand on his arm or risk bumping him. "I cheated," Hazel whispered.

He raised his eyebrows. "Oh?"

"I had a good luck charm," she revealed.

Mack leaned forward as she did. Silence surrounded them as their mouths touched. Their kiss spoke to her of sacrifices garnering reward, of unconditional love and acceptance, and of a future where she could teach others like her to find strength in family. His lips caressed hers before he pulled back.

Sounds suddenly closed around her again, and she looked at the crowd then back to Mack. His fingers caressed her cheek at the astonishment that crossed her face. "What was that about?"

Closing her eyes, she placed her hand over his and nuzzled into his palm. "Oh, Mack, I've found my quiet place. It's with you."

ABOUT THE AUTHOR

Thia Mackin was born halfway between Jim Beam and the Bourbon Capital of the World in Samuels, Kentucky. As such, she loves everything about Bourbon—except the taste—and will happily take her guests on a few of the distillery tours so they can decide their preference for themselves. Nothing smells like home as much as sour mash fumes from the many local distilleries permeating the air.

An avid reader and writer, she enjoys traveling to new places—both real and imaginary. The Caribbean Sea holds her heart, though she'll accept any ocean as a stand-in on short notice. The only drawback to traveling is leaving behind her four-legged family members—her Rottweiler name Luc and her cats named Tipsy and Mustachio.

facebook.com/AuthorThiaMackin
instagram.com/mackinaroundtheworld
twitter.com/thiamackin

LET'S GET SOCIAL

Follow co-creator Kat Corley on Facebook www.
facebook.com/katcorleywrites/!
Find me on TikTok: www.tiktok.com/@thiamackin

If you would like to discuss the world of Midnight Rising,
please join our Facebook group
Thia and Kat's Midnight Readers.

Visit **www.ThiaMackin.com**
Thank you for visiting. We hope you stay!
~ Thia

SNEAK PEEK OF TEQUILA MOON

CHAPTER 1

While I didn't subscribe to the saying that the best way to get to know a new town was through a bar fight, I rather enjoyed saying hello to one with a stiff drink. Normally, I chose the place myself—and Eiffel Creek, Colorado, hadn't made my list. Unfortunately, my Toyota 4Runner had other plans.

When the thermostat edged quickly toward overheating a couple hours after sunset, I pulled into a deserted gas station parking lot and popped the hood to a cloud of steam. My hand subconsciously patted the roof in reassurance before I went to the hatch to grab the toolbox and flashlight. The split in the hose didn't take long to find and not much longer to remove.

"Not funny, Sparky," I grumbled at the six-year-old vehicle.

A glance around revealed a well-lit building about a mile down the road. In under a minute, four cars pulled in. The headlights shone on a small wood-sided building, not much different than the business I stood in front of—except that one wasn't closed. At nine p.m., I doubted this blink-and-I'd-miss-it town had a parts store open.

I closed the hood and walked to the back, tossing the busted hose inside. Flipping the flashlight to off and putting the toolbox back in the rear hatch, I pulled out a few baby wipes to clean my hands as best I could. Grease rarely cooperated. Tonight wasn't an exception; black wedged under most of my fingernails. Grumpy, I slammed the door shut so hard the license plate shuddered. "Sorry, baby," I murmured to the wagon, still frustrated but exhaling loudly to expel the pissed off.

Weighing my options left me leaning hard toward a walk. I needed a bathroom, food, and a shot of tequila or four. And I would happily cheat by Gating—using energy to create a door between the places—if the likelihood of cameras at one business or the other wasn't pretty high. Besides, maybe I'd be a mite less aggravated when I arrived if I powered myself there on my own steam.

After a quick stop to grab my purse from the passenger seat, I hit the key fob to lock the doors and set a brisk pace toward the lights down the road. The air smelled of dying leaves and snowflakes falling on the peak of the mountains in the distance. If I didn't hate the cold so much, perhaps it would be pretty. Rubbing my arms through my light jacket, I quickened my steps to a half-hearted jog.

A spotlight illuminated the words The Howling Moon on the wooden sign out front, and the name shone in blue on the side of the building. The third o was actually shaped like a crescent moon with a wolf—muzzle to the sky—in the break. My eyes rolled hard enough it hurt.

"C'mon. Clichéd much?"

Though my mutter would be impossible to hear inside over the rock music and din of voices, I momentarily felt bad for saying it. People used what worked, and the name didn't

106 | THIA MACKIN

deter anyone if the dozen cars in the parking lot was any indicator.

My hand smoothed over my auburn hair, feeling the flyaways but unable to do anything to tame them. Today had just been a travel day, so I'd gone for comfortable. My jeans were well-worn, and my faded shirt showed the double yellow lines of a highway with the Susan Sontag quotation, "I haven't been everywhere, but it's on my list." Plus, my hiking boots could have used a good scrub after my last adventure.

At least my cash spends.

I slipped inside with a thank-you when an incoming patron held the door open, taking a step to the side to orient myself. Though the music had sounded uncomfortably loud from the outside, I could still hear myself think inside. In fact, if I concentrated, I could make out the conversation at the table closest to me. I tuned them out. No need to be rude when they didn't deserve it.

Two robust dart stations were set up in one corner, neither in use. However, all four of the billiards tables enjoyed healthy Friday night crowds. The well-lit area showed quarters lined up as people claimed a spot playing the winner. It appeared that a few of the stacks of coins had a bill or two underneath as a bet. If the repair became too expensive, I could make some gas money back tomorrow night.

All but a couple tables had customers gathered around them. Luckily, only two people were at the bar—the bartender and the man he handed two beers. The patron tilted the top of one bottle toward him before hurrying back to the table where a pretty brunette waited. That left plenty of room for me to grab a bar stool and toss back a couple drinks before heading back to Sparky to sleep. If I were really lucky, the Howling Moon would offer at least a couple fried food options to get me through until morning.

"Hello, Red," the bartender greeted immediately, having watched me approach and remove my jacket. His honey-colored eyes, perfectly arched eyebrows, and carefully tousled and gelled hair spoke of a man who knew he looked damn good. Probably, he had a place nearby to take the ladies he picked up for a one-night stand. I had worked with dozens of players like him. Shit, I even liked most of them. I would never, ever fuck one, though. "What would you like?"

Gritting my teeth, I forced myself to smile sweetly then chose the seat that allowed me the best view of the room. I set my jacket on the stool beside me. "You to never call me 'Red' again, to start. Also, a double shot of tequila."

His lips twitched, apparently unperturbed by my attitude. "I'm Miguel. What would you like me to call you?"

"A cab after I'm well and truly drunk, but you have to serve me a drink first," I reminded, gesturing toward the row of golden liquor as he leaned on the counter, in no hurry to pour my drink. After a long moment of us staring at each other, I sighed. "I'm not here to flirt, Miguel. I'm thirsty."

An even voice from behind the bar interjected, "Good thing you found the bar, then. Everything else in town closed an hour ago."

Two shot glasses appeared in front of me, the hand that placed them there disappearing so quickly I didn't catch a glimpse of the second bartender's face. However, his appearance hadn't only surprised me. Miguel jumped. Somehow, that made me feel better.

"Fucking dude. Rafferty, make some noise next time," Miguel groused, his entire attitude changing as he stood up straight. He stabbed two limes with a martini pick and set them on a plate in front of me before wiping down the already spotless countertop.

Rafferty knelt in front of a small fridge, his back to us. He restocked the contents from the box he had apparently

108 | THIA MACKIN

carried in one arm while pouring and delivering two shots of tequila to me. As a mixed-bag demon with above-human strength and reflexes who'd spent my last fifteen years working in bars, I wasn't sure I could have accomplished the feat without spilling anything. Color me impressed.

I tossed back the first tequila, enjoying the familiar burn as the contents hit my stomach. Then I set my elbow on the bar and watched the closest table of billiards. The two demons—I couldn't tell if they were human or another breed—played eight-ball, the classic solids and stripes. Evenly matched, they kept pranking and distracting each other as they made their way around the table. Most people would have ended up in a brawl, but they never even looked at each other sideways.

"Did you need a menu or were you able to catch a restaurant before everything closed for the night?" the voice from earlier asked.

I turned, looking up to meet his startling blue-gray eyes. Unlike Miguel, this man hadn't spent more time in front of the mirror than I did in a week. He was tidy and handsome but not glamorous or model perfect. For example, he'd combed his hair, but he hadn't styled it. Also, his question held no flirtation. Maybe a little concern, though.

"A menu would be fantastic," I answered honestly. "Thank you."

He slid a laminated, five-by-seven paper across the bar. "Your choices are basically fried, fried, or fried."

"Excellent." I skimmed the list. "Bacon cheeseburger with mozzarella sticks, please. Also, another tequila, a little salt, with a water back."

He scribbled my food order on a piece of paper, handing it to Miguel when he stepped back behind the bar with a tray of empty beer bottles and glasses.

BEAR HUG | 109

"Thanks, Boss," the surly flirt grumbled, pushing through the swinging door into the kitchen.

A moment later, the empty shot glass disappeared and had been replaced with a full, salt-rimmed one and a glass of ice water. When I glanced up to thank him, he had moved down the counter, efficiently popped the tops on six beers, and carried them to a table in the middle of the room. Someone flagged him at another high top, and he grinned at whatever the customer said. Dropping into the seat across from the guy, he set his elbow on the table. The other man clasped his hand, mirroring his pose. After a couple long seconds, Rafferty slammed the man's wrist against the table.

Wolf whistles and applause filled that half of the room, and if my vision wasn't failing me, a faint blush crept up the winner's neck. However, his back turned to me as he collected the empties from a couple tables before heading through the swinging door.

Heels clicked purposefully up behind me, stopping a couple feet away. Taking the second shot, I squeezed one of the limes directly into my mouth. I dropped the rind in the empty glass and turned around.

"You're new," the woman observed, not unkindly. "I'm Hazel Metcalf."

She stuck out her hand for me to shake, and I accepted it warily, knowing my Gift operated on touch. Luckily, only the tiniest zap of energy passed between us, like a spark of static electricity, before she slid onto the stool on the opposite side of me as my jacket. Whatever my Gift had set in motion for her, it would be a minor mishap or win. That meant her current karmic scales had been pretty balanced, and the consequence of our touch would fully even it out.

"I arrived in town less than an hour ago," I agreed. "Karma Delaney."

She swung her foot and grinned. "Welcome to Eiffel

110 | THIA MACKIN

Creek, Karma! We're a town of 740 people, so it isn't difficult to pick out a new face."

I heard the swinging door move but didn't look to see which bartender came out. "How come you give her your name and not me?" Miguel asked, not sounding as grumpy as his words suggested. He slid a basket with a massive burger and generous order of mozzarella sticks in front of me.

"Hazel was genuine and friendly, not a practiced flirt," I explained.

He took a moment to process it. "Fair. Hey, Hazelbear. I accidentally dropped onion rings first instead of mozz. Want a free order?"

That was quick. As expected, the effect of our touch had been small, but the little positive made me like her more as she thanked him profusely.

He asked if we needed condiments, and we agreed on ketchup before he headed back to get it. As soon as he went through the door, Hazel dropped a few dollars into the tip jar. I wanted an excuse to brush against her again so she could reap the reward for being a sweet person. Instead, I bit into the burger. Surprised by how delicious it tasted, I closed my eyes to savor it better.

Hazel laughed in delight. "Right? They use fresh ground beef. Rafferty has his own secret blend of spices to season it. I hear it's the only place worth getting a burger in town."

When Miguel stepped out, I gave him a thumbs-up, and he paused mid-step in confusion before handing Hazel the basket of onion rings and bottle of ketchup.

"She likes the sandwich," my new friend explained, squeezing a mound of red onto the checkered paper. In response, he bowed to me then slid Hazel an IPA. She removed the screw-top lid and sipped before daintily biting into an onion ring smothered in Heinz. When she slid the ketchup to me, I passed. It would be a shame to ruin the burger's flavor.

"How long are you staying?"

I shrugged a shoulder and finished chewing. "It depends. How long do you think it will take me to get a replacement hose for my Toyota?"

She frowned. "Oh no."

I shrugged again, having already mentally done the math after she told me the town's population. "Monday, I take it?"

Her frown lines deepened. "Monday is Labor Day."

"Then Tuesday." I preferred to not sleep in Sparky for four nights without a shower. "Do you know anywhere within walking distance that I could grab a shower Sunday?"

She offered me an onion ring, and I traded her a mozzarella stick. "Everywhere is walking distance here, if you don't mind a hike. Main Street is only a mile long if you start from here, and from the center of town to the creek is just under five miles. But we don't have a lot of visitors in Eiffel Creek. Miss Grace rents out her guest suite sometimes, but she went to visit family out of state for the long weekend." Her face lit up for a second. "I can let you in at the gym, though. I planned to go in Sunday for some after-hours cleaning, and you can use the shower there!"

At cruising speed of seventy miles per hour, I truly would have missed even noticing the tiny town if Sparky hadn't run hot. Three minutes and gone. Now, I had to camp here for the weekend and shower on the goodwill of a friendly stranger to keep from stinking up my home-on-the-road.

Dammit, Sparky, couldn't you have broken down near a thriving truck stop?

"I appreciate that, Hazel. You won't get in trouble, will you?"

She waved away my concern, her eyes twinkling. "I own the gym, so definitely not. If there was a place more comfort-

112 | THIA MACKIN

able to sleep than a treadmill or the concrete floor, I'd offer to let you stay there."

I grinned. "I sleep in the Toyota a lot. The roads call to me if I stay any place long, and hotels are too expensive. The back seat and a well-lit truck stop are my home. What time Sunday? And is it on Main Street?"

"I'll be there eight a.m. to lunch. You just stop by whenever. Follow the main road here down a quarter mile, and it is on the left... Unless you'd rather I pick you up?" she offered, her expression earnest enough that I patted her hand. This time, the zap between us was a little stronger. I hoped something great happened to her.

"No, thank you. The walk will do me good."

She beamed at me, laying her empty beer bottle in the empty basket and piling her garbage on top. "It has been so wonderful to meet you, Karma. We have nearly double the men here in Eiffel Creek than women, and it gets crazy lonely at times."

"I am looking forward to seeing you Sunday. Is there somewhere I could buy you lunch after for the trouble?"

"We can go to The Diner. They serve breakfast all day on Sundays. Best biscuits and gravy in a hundred miles," she gushed.

From the tables, someone yelled her name. "You're up, Hazelbear!"

She grinned. "Gotta go kick his patootie. See you Sunday!"

I shook my head as she darted across the room. Stacking my empty basket under hers, I followed her example and cleaned up as much as I could. Then I dropped a ten in the tip jar and headed toward the bathroom, which was clean enough to eat off the floors. I'd been in hundreds—literally hundreds—of bars, and this one was easily the cleanest ever.

"Ready for your check and that cab, Karma?" Miguel

asked when I came back to the bar, all hints of his earlier flirting gone.

I smiled at him, glad he could still learn. Of course, he'd probably poured on the charm because I was a new face in a small town. All the other girls knew his tricks. "Check, yes. Cab, no. It's a short walk, and the food soaked up most of the liquor."

While I waited for him to cash me out, I surreptitiously looked around for the more handsome bartender. *Rafferty.* Perhaps he was still in the back doing inventory? I mentally chided myself for being upset at not seeing him.

"He's already headed out," Miguel murmured, handing me my change. His eyes laughed at me, but his expression stayed customer-service friendly.

"Who?" I asked, raising a brow in question.

He grinned. "Stop back in tomorrow. I'll buy your first shot."

Slipping my jacket back on, I waved at Hazel before taking a last glance behind the bar. "Have a good night, Miguel."

When I stepped out, the temperature had dropped. Zipping my jacket, I tucked my head and started toward the truck. Though my steps were silent, a click-click-click followed me. The sound doubled my heartrate, and I turned around to walk backwards.

A big white dog followed at a safe distance. It looked like a massive white German Shepherd, maybe mixed with a Great Pyrenees. I might have thought it was a wolf if it wouldn't have been the biggest damn wolf I'd ever seen. Also, most wolves wouldn't perk their ears at me and wag their tail when I faced them.

"Hey, big guy. You startled me," I told him—at least I assumed it was a him as big as it was—keeping my voice calm as I continued walking backwards down the road. Just in case his jaws had enough strength to puncture the energy shield that protected me, I slipped off my jacket and wrapped it around my left arm. It would protect my skin if he attacked.

His tail wagged harder, and his tongue lolled in a doggie grin. However, he didn't attempt to close the distance between us, following along as though we were just going in the same direction.

When I reached the Toyota, I clicked the unlock button on the fob. I stopped, waiting to see what the dog did before turning my back to get in. He sat down, his tail still moving. After a moment, I took a step toward him. "Are you a good boy or am I going to regret this?" I asked him, my right hand extended palm up.

He bounced in place, obviously excited at the potential attention. I grinned, no teeth, as I remembered that showing teeth could be seen as a sign of aggression in canids. "Please be a good boy," I whispered, holding my palm in front of him.

Sniffing my hand, he licked it before staring up at me expectantly. I took the hint and rubbed the damp palm on his head. "Oh shit. You're soft." My fingers caressed his warm ears then ran through the thick fur at his scruff. "You're a very good boy. And you obviously have a family somewhere, because you look too healthy and clean for a stray."

His white fur almost gleamed in the dark.

"Thanks for the love, handsome. Now go on home. It's dangerous for a lone doggie to be wandering this late. Colorado has wolves, bears, and coyotes... all kinds of things."

He barked as I moved away, and I sighed. "I'm serious. Go home, buddy."

After a moment, he stood and walked toward the abandoned gas station. Hopefully, his house was that way. I opened the back of the Toyota, found my gallon of water, and brushed my teeth quickly. Tossing my blankets and pillows into the backseat, I shut the hatch and climbed inside. Locking the doors, I curled up across the backseat. For the first few minutes, I shivered. Then my heat became trapped between the blankets. The windows fogged up as the temperature went up inside the cab, and I closed my eyes.

This was going to be a long weekend.